THE GEM STATE SIEGE

AJ McMullen

The Gem State Siege

Copyright © 2021 Ascension Media Group

All rights reserved. No part of this publication may be reproduced, distributed, or transmitted in any form or by any means, including photocopying, recording, or other electronic or mechanical methods, without the prior written permission of the publisher, except in the case of brief quotations embodied in critical reviews and certain other non-commercial uses prohibited by copyright law. For permission requests, write to the publisher, addressed "Attention: Permissions Coordinator." At the address below.

ISBN: 978-1-955254-00-7 (Paperback)
ISBN: 978-1-955254-01-4 (Ebookbook)

Any reference to historical events, people, and places are used fictitiously.fictitious. Names, characters, and places are products of the author's imagination.

Cover image and design by Evocative.
First printing edition 2021

www.ajmcmullen.com

The Gem State Siege

Dedication

This book, in part, is dedicated to an old friend. One who used to make me laugh and smile anytime I visited his store. There is not a day I don't recall your jokes from behind your cash register. Hope you are at peace, Abdul.

This book is also dedicated to those of you that have dreams to do more in life. Your destiny is written in the stars, not on the ground, so keep your head up.

The Gem State Siege

<u>Acknowledgments</u>

There have been days where I wanted nothing more than to finish what I started. But there were more days where I felt I could not continue. On these days, the people in my life helped me stay focused and persistent. So I say thanks. To everyone that cheered me on from afar, and to those who didn't. Because all of you played a part in why I kept going. I say thanks to everyone in Ascension Media for either believing in me or not, either way, you said kind words that helped me keep pushing. I want to thank the love of my life. Alyssa, you helped me keep pushing through the worst of times. When I thought I couldn't do it, you helped me move to the next word, the next read, and the next revision. Now we are here. I love you. May we all grow together, fore this is only one piece of our legacy fulfilled. This is only the beginning

The Gem State Siege

CHAPTER I

This is where your story starts. I will not diminish what you have gone through... yet. It was a tragedy, but what is coming is the real tragedy.

You want to know who I am? I could tell you I'm just a young man from Idaho Falls. Unfortunately, in this story, I'm much more. I am the one who may be responsible for all this madness. But I'm not sure what to think anymore. I know that what's happening now seems to have a lot to do with what happened then, back in 2021.

A man who was once the villain told me a tale I now believe is the catalyst to this tragedy. A story, if altered at the moment, could have led me to live a normal life. But I cannot be sure of the outcomes from the conversation that morning in the White House.

He sat in the Oval Office that day as the Chief of Staff. He was in the presence of Vice-President Hawthorne McTierman and President, Nathaniel Wesley.

"How did this happen?"

"Mr. President, we are told this is a result of a weaponized biochemical designed to be used as leverage for war."

"War? What war are you referring to exactly?"

"Mr. President—"

"And who the hell authorized biochemical research?"

"I don't know, Sir. But I can get that answer for you."

Angry, red in the face and undoing his necktie, the President stood from his desk and stared intensely at Allan Waddell.

The Gem State Siege

Vice-President McTierman sat on a sofa just yards away from the President's desk with his legs crossed. He stared at the glass of scotch in his hand and pretended not to listen to the conversation.

"You seem awfully quiet during all of this, Hawthorne," said the President.

"Yeah, I'm just as shocked about this."

The towering man walked around his desk with a manila folder in hand. He approached a coffee table placed between two sofas, slammed the folder down next to a glass decanter, and paced the floor.

"Did you do this?"

"Now, Mr. President, you know that is—"

"Hawthorne, this is a tragedy that will upend the lives of us all!"

The President sat down on the sofa across from him and locked eyes. Hawthorne cleared his throat, intimidated by the war veteran.

"Mr. President, I am aware. But, I assure you, this is not my doing."

The men got quiet as the President stared down at the folder with the red classified tape across the top. McTierman looked up at Waddell as if he was signaling him.

"Mr. President, you want answers, then that is what you will get. Allow me the opportunity to gather the intel you need." Said Waddell.

"Is that our only option? Standby and wait for the answers to be thrown at us?"

"Sir, I have a team of people who will be able to dig in places at the bottom that we are too high to reach. Let me go to them. It is the only way to fix this."

The President seemed wary of the plan, but it was all he had at the moment. There was not even a suspect on his list to point out.

"What do you need from us, Mr. Waddell?"

"Mr. Vice-President, sir, all I would need is one of you to sign off on the work of an outside source to track this group down." Vice-President McTierman looked up at his commander-in-chief, seeing the despair in his eyes.

"Wes," he called out, almost snapping him out of a trance. "We will figure this out. Don't you worry."

McTierman looked up at Waddell and gave him a nod of approval. Waddell nodded back, then looked down at the President.

"You find me whatever organization that is responsible for this, and you have their asses front and center in this office."

"Yes, Mr. President, Sir!"

Waddell walked around the sofa behind the President and headed towards the exit. But, not before getting a signal from the Vice-President.

The door opened to reveal the bustling halls of the White House, then it closed. He said the Nation's Capital never seemed so busy. Members of the Secret Service stood by the door. One reached inside the office to close it after Waddell exited.

The Gem State Siege

CHAPTER II

Months later, something happened in Idaho Falls that would be a result of the conversation in the White House. February, a month that would usually be frigid in the Gem State. Normally, weeks without sunshine and snow piled up to the side of roads and parking lots would be expected. But, the temperature on this day was 112 degrees Fahrenheit. I remember seeing this on my mom's car dashboard while we were sitting in traffic on the I-15. Mom had said something during the fall months about her car's air conditioning malfunctioning. She couldn't possibly see weather like this on the forecast to get it fixed beforehand. We were forced to ride with the windows down for air. I remember that day so vividly as the air was foul from all the running vehicles around us. I remember having an inability to breathe and being so uncomfortable I cried for my mom to take me home.

My mother ignored me as she was on the phone with my father, complaining about how he never came home. She was so upset I could see her veins popping up from her forehead as she yelled into the Bluetooth speaker. I could hear my father's voice yelling back at her with confusion set in his tone because he did not know what to do about the situation at the moment. I never believed my father was a bad guy. I remember the two of them arguing and fighting a lot more during this time. But, I was still too young to understand why.

My childhood was spent mostly with my mother because my dad spent it working. I never perceived my mother to have a job because she was always home. My dad is a geologist, and he travels for his work. It wasn't his fault that he spent so much time away from home. He had a job that always pulled him back to his office, wherever it was at that moment. It was not rare for him to spend his vacation time to keep working because that is what his boss demanded. Their current argument started during a disagreement about my upcoming sixth birthday. But there was unusual seismic activity happening nationwide. My dad's company did its best to investigate and understand. That's what we were all told anyway.

"Milo, you have to reason with me and at least meet me halfway."

"Tawnie, I am not sure what you want from me."

Angry at his lack of compliance, my mother snapped again.

"Got dammit, Milo, I am sick of this!"

"Mommy, it's too hot!" I screamed from the back seat, trying to interrupt my parents.

"I know, honey. We will be home in a little while." She said to satiate me. Immediately, she and my dad were back to arguing.

"With everything going on with the seismic activity, I am needed on the case more than ever." My dad pleaded.

"Why does it always have to be you?"

"It is the burden of being the lead researcher in the area."

"I don't understand what I'm supposed to do, Milo."

"Mommy, mommy!" I screamed again. Frustrated at my constant outbursts, she turned around to scold me for being rude. On the other end, my father made another remark that suggested he disapproved of my mother's parenting method.

"What was that?"

"He's just a kid, Tawnie. You do not have to yell at him

like that," he said to her. She dropped her head for a moment and began to shake due to anger.

After a few seconds of being silent on the line, my mother exploded at him once more. I immediately started to cry out.

"How dare you try to give me parenting advice!" she yelled. The people in the other cars stared because she was now acting like a psychopath. They screamed back and forth for about five minutes until her phone died.

"Shit, shit, shit!" she yelled as she had a temper tantrum in the front seat of the car. Unable to speak in this stressful moment, I whimpered in the back seat. In fear that she would lose her temper at me the same way, I stayed silent.

She turned to tend to me in the rear seat with tears in her eyes. "Baby, mommy's sorry!"

She spent a few minutes trying to calm me down and wiped the sweat from me with a hand towel that she had next to her.

"Lady, everything okay?" a man from a truck next to us asked her.

"Yeah." My timid mother answered him as she turned back around and faced the front. The guy made small talk, and the two of them joked about the heat and traffic jam for a moment.

"I wonder what's stopping us right now. It's never usually this bad, right?" he asked.

"No, it's not."

"It can't possibly get any worse than this, right?"

"Wait, don't say that!" my mother laughed. "That's usually when it does."

After the two of them laughed together about her joke, the

man finally turned his attention to me in the back seat.

"Hey there, little man!" he said. He was a young, white male that sported a baseball cap and a lot of peach fuzz as if he hadn't shaved in weeks. He sat higher than us in a tall pickup truck. This prevented me from sliding down in my seat and disappearing from his view. So I did the only thing I knew to do. As my car window rolled up, the man laughed. My mom looked back at me with her mouth wide open.

"Milo?" she called out in surprise.

"No, it's fine. That just means you're raising him well." The man said.

"Thank you for saying that."

The two talked for a few more minutes and the heat made me roll down my window once more. This was the very moment that it all started.

"Mom!" I called out for her attention."

Instead of acknowledging me, she continued her conversation with the strange man.

"Mom, mom!" I called out again.

"Milo, hang on," she said as she held her finger up to me. Getting frustrated at her ignoring me, I exploded and screamed for her at the top of my lungs.

"MILO?" she answered with concern.

"Mom, what is that?!"

"Wait, what?" She looked around.

"Something's coming! Something's coming, mommy!" I panicked, unsure of what I was feeling. I pulled at the straps on my booster seat and tried to open the car door.

She reached for me, "Milo, Milo, calm down! Relax." She glanced over at the man in the truck with embarrassment on her face, and he just smiled and waited.

But as I stared at the man, I noticed as he turned to look in front of him. In front of us was a semi-truck trailer that my mother couldn't see around. But, the man in the tall pickup could see over most of the cars in the traffic jam. His expression changed, his mouth fell open as he did not understand whatever he was seeing.

"What the hell?" he asked. My mom looked at me with wide eyes and moved her left hand down to unbuckle herself. I took that opportunity to open the car door. As I jumped out, I could hear my mother calling for me. But I ran as fast as I could between the vehicles in the traffic jam. Concerned people called out for me as I ran past their open windows. But, I was not going to stop until I got away from whatever I was feeling.

Mom got out of the car as the ground underneath us began to tremor. As she looked over to the man in the truck, the two of them made eye contact. A loud crackling sound preceded his truck falling as the ground underneath became unstable. She ran around the front of her car and saw his entire lane had sunk. The man was now at eye level with my mom's pedicured toes and panicked as he was now unable to exit his vehicle. She stepped back as she looked down in fear as the pieces of the road disintegrated, pulling her in as well. The fissure was growing. Explosions up ahead were throwing and incinerating cars. Upbursts of flames followed the cracks in the ground and headed towards her. My mom tuned everything else out and ran behind me.

"MILO!" she yelled out to me. At this point, everyone who had the wherewithal to comprehend what was happening had jumped out of their vehicles. I was bumped around as the adults showed extreme disregard to me. To avoid being trampled, I rolled under a semi-truck and waited for another opportunity to jump back into the panicking crowd. In fear that I would be flattened, I stayed under the truck and watched the cracks in the road spread underneath me. I could see red light radiating from the ground as it got hotter. As the crowd started to thin out, my mother crouched down next to the truck and called out to me. She had her arm extended and blood running down her face.

"Milo, come on!" she screamed as I could see a bright light shining from behind her. I reached out for her hand, she yanked me back to her and ran through the cars with me draped over her shoulder.

I watched the chaos unfolding behind her as a wall of flames blasted into the sky, and the I-15 fell into the Earth. But somehow, we were able to escape the scorching flames and cracks in the ground. I remember opening my eyes, and we were far away from the devastation, watching it from a distance. My mother got me to a safe space, put me down on the ground, and collapsed as she panted for air. I examined our surroundings as I stood back up, trying to comprehend how we got here so fast. We were about a mile away from where we were. It felt like only seconds had passed. How did that happen? Black smoke filled the skies above and almost blocked out the sun, and I felt cold air blow through the city for a moment. But almost instantly, it was hot again. I looked back at my mom, who was now sobbing and trying to get back up. I ran over to help her, and she wrapped her arms around me and pulled me tight. I wish I could say it was over. But, this was only the beginning.

CHAPTER III

Mass panic surrounded. Emergency vehicles filled the streets, restricting access to the disaster. The paramedics set up a first aid outpost near the blockades for the injured. A police officer found my mom and me near the highway. My mom, at this point, was unconscious and had trouble breathing, so he brought us to the facility. I cried as the men wrangled my defenseless little mother like a rag doll, tossing her body where they needed it. A paramedic attempted to calm me down and hold me back as I watched them, scared that I would never see her again.

"Mommy!" I screamed until my throat was sore. But no matter how much I called, the men in blue jumpsuits blocked my vision of her. Everything seemed like it was in slow motion as they appeared to start beating her. I began to hyperventilate, not knowing what to do. I felt the urge to run away again. People all around me talked, but I could hear nothing. A paramedic yelled, "She's okay!"

The room was noisy enough to compromise my senses. But that is the only thing I heard over the commotion. Though still chaotic around us, our section grew calm. A paramedic turned around and called for me to come over. I was hesitant to move, unsure of what he would say to me.

"Your mommy needs your help." I ran over to the cot, and he took a knee to talk to me.

"What's your name, kid?"

"Milo," I responded as I wiped my eyes with my forearms.

"Okay, Milo, here's what I need you to do, buddy. I was

hoping you could call out to your mommy to wake her up. Can you do that?" I nodded before he could even finish his statement.

"Once she's up, you have to make sure that she doesn't go back to sleep. Okay?"

Immediately, I grabbed my mom's limp hand and began to scream out for her.

"Mommy, mommy!"

As I did that, I sensed something odd happening around us. Everyone in attendance was now fixated on us. Everyone whispered, and surprise covered their faces as they looked on. She squeezed my hand. It was a bit weak at first, but as I continued to call out for her, "Mommy, mommy," her grip became tighter as she opened her eyes. I was so excited. My mother reached up with her other hand and pulled off the oxygen mask from her face.

"Dr. Simms?" One paramedic called out.

"I thought she looked familiar," said another.

Someone ran over to my mother with a wet towel to treat the wound on the side of her head and clean the dust from her face. They all seemed to know her already and talked amongst one another. How do they know my mom? Soon after she was awake, the staff rushed us out of the tent. They needed room for those who still had injuries from the disaster. Holding on to her head as she got up from the rickety cot, she groaned as she propped herself up to a vertical position. She let go of my hand and grabbed her belongings.

"Milo, we have to go," She said to me, looking around the tent with sharp eyes.

"But mommy!" I called out, concerned for her well-being.

"Milo!"

She looked down at me as she stood up from the cot. It wasn't but a second before a police officer walked over to my mother with a serious look on his face.

"Ma'am. I am Deputy Sheriff Boulevardez, and I was hoping for a statement of what you saw today."

She looked frightened look as she reached for my shoulder and pulled me towards her.

"Hi, officer," she said to acknowledge the man. "I don't know how much help I could be right now."

"I understand. You may still be in shock from what happened. I understand that you inhaled a lot of smoke. So you could still be a little hazy on the things that took place today. But I promise you, every little bit helps us understand what happened out there today. Loved ones were lost."

"Okay. I understand." She spoke softly as she gripped my shoulder.

"Why don't you start by telling me where you were when this all started?" The officer took out a black notepad from his shirt pocket and clicked a pen.

"I was on I-15 between exits 118 and 19." She said to him.

"That was right there, at the epicenter. What did you see exactly? How did you notice it?"

I looked up at her. A brief expression of concern showed in her eyes as she stared down at me. I started to feel like I was in trouble.

"I just felt the earthquake and got out of my car to see what was going on." She said as she looked around for a moment in suspicion.

"Okay, do you know anything else that would help us figure out what happened out there, Dr. Simms?"

"I am going to go out on a limb and say that the random

traffic jam may be a contributing factor to what happened."

The officer raised an eyebrow and stopped writing for a second, then he asked, "Why do you say that?"

"It isn't rare for a two-lane highway to get backed up with traffic, but today was not normal," she explained.

The officer gave her a look that seemed odd for the context of the situation. It was almost as if he had become suspicious of her.

"You know what, officer?" she said as she rounded up the rest of her belongings.

"Due to the concussion, I am a bit hazy, as a matter of fact. I also need to go and check on my family."

The officer closed his notepad and smiled.

"Of course, Dr. Simms. Is there anything I could do for you at this moment?" he asked. My mom nudged me along as he kept his eyes on us the entire time.

"No, I think we will be okay once we get as far away from the chaos as possible." We headed towards the exit.

"You take care now," the officer yelled as we left.

As we walked down the road, my mother pulled her phone out and began to dial.

"Milo, stay close, please, honey!" she yelled for me as she looked back to make sure I was behind her.

"Mommy," I called out. "Where is daddy?"

"I don't know, honey. I'm going to try and call right now. I'm just not sure if I have enough battery to turn it on."

"Okay." I timidly said to her. "I hope he's okay."

"Me too, honey."

We walked for a bit longer before reaching a nearby shopping center. People gathered to watch the incident from a safe distance.

"Oh no!" my mom said.

"What?" I asked, thinking that something was wrong. "Is daddy okay?"

"I don't know yet, Milo. My phone won't turn on."

She scanned the shopping center across the road from where we stood with acute focus.

"Come on, Milo." She said as she grabbed my hand and pulled me along.

"I'm glad I got my phone out of the car, but I'm kicking myself for not making sure to charge it."

We walked across the street to a gas station that my mom usually goes to. Out in front were several cruiser motorcycles. She stopped to look at them with concern. That is when she squeezed my hand and walked me into the store. We went straight to the charging cables. A television was on behind the counter at the front of the store. It was no surprise that it showed the breaking news coverage. My mother grabbed the cable and headed to the clerk. She stood there, waiting for the Arabic man to address her. But he and a few other patrons gawked at the television program.

"How could something like this happen?" The clerk asked.

"I bet it's some government experiment that went wrong. You know how that is." Another man added.

The group of men stopped their conversation. They stood there mesmerized by the broadcast on television. One man turned around and raised an eyebrow when he saw us. Uncomfortable with the bearded, tattooed man, my mom placed her hand on my head. We crept backward as he stared at us. The man looked down and saw me staring up at him. He then looked at his friends and nodded. They left the store without causing any trouble for us. We stepped forward to the counter, and I could see a single tear and great pain in mom's eyes. Her body twitching and shivering in fear. I reached up and took her hand, and she looked down and gave me a big grin as if nothing was wrong at all. At the time, I had no idea what she was going through. All I could do was be a good boy because she was on edge, and the last thing I wanted was for her to be upset with me.

"Those damn Shiners!" She blurted.

"They are some bad people." The store clerk responded with his thick Indian accent.

"I wonder what would have happened if Milo wasn't with me?"

"Dr. Simms, the world is falling apart outside. Racism is on vacation. Know what I mean? Don't let it bother you!"

"Yeah, I'll try."

The store clerk got quiet and looked down at me. He looked back up to my mom and tilted his head to the side as he tried to get a better look at her.

"You look like shit."

My mother dropped her head and began to chuckle for a moment.

"Yeah, I feel like it too, Abdul," she responded with a smile.

"Were you there?" my mom nodded as she continued to stare at the news. "Oh, man!"

The camera switched to an aerial view of the aftermath. A giant pit formed on the west side of Idaho Falls and completely engulfed that side of the city. According to reporters on the scene, the hole was about two miles wide, and there was no seeing the bottom. It was so scary that we almost ended up at the bottom of that.

"You keep smiling and keep your head up. I'm glad you're okay."

"Thank you," my mom said with a teary smile.

"Boy, take care of your mama, you hear me? She a good woman." The store owner yelled at me. I hardly understood what he said.

"Y... yes, sir," I answered.

My mom and I walked out of the store and headed to the side of the building. I remained quiet as my mother scurried, looking for something on the ground and the walls. I could see the frustration growing in her demeanor.

"Shit!" She yelled.

She grabbed my hand and took me across the street to a department store and looked around there as well. When we got there, she got excited as she opened the charger packaging to plug into her phone. She crouched down at the wall and plugged the phone into an outlet. As we waited for the phone to charge, she finally began to unravel. I stayed quiet and allowed her time to let out her frustrations. I watched people move about the city around us. People rushing in and out of the store with groceries and supplies as they prepared for the end of the world.

"Milo," she called out to me with her head in her hands. "Can you tell mommy something?"

"Yes, mommy?" I answered her.

"How did you know that was about to happen?"

"I... I" I struggled to get the words out.

"Did you feel it?" she asked me with fear in her expression. Without answering her, I nodded my head.

She bit her bottom lip and looked up to the sky as she sighed. The next question she asked me did not make sense at that moment. But as I grew older, I came to understand exactly why she asked me.

"Milo did you... Did you do this?"

I shook my head, dreading the idea of her thinking I could do this.

"No, it wasn't me, mommy! I swear!" I yelled as tears rushed down my face. She reached out and pulled me close to her, and hugged me.

"What did you feel?" she asked.

"I thought it was a monster," I answered. "It's coming to get us because we hurt it."

"What exactly is... it?"

"The spirit."

Upon saying this, one could have assumed that I dusted chalkboard erasers on my mom's face. She had become so flushed with fear that her skin seemed to lose its color. After staring at me for a moment, wondering about what I told her, she decided to give the phone another try. Optimistic, she dialed through to my dad. With each ring, I could see her face seeming less confident about reaching him. Once the call went to voice-mail, my mother hid her face from me as her eyes became glossy. I could do nothing but hug her and tell her that everything would be okay. She turned me around and sat down on the ground with me in her lap. We sat there, waiting and watching the world around us fall apart.

CHAPTER IV

After my mom's phone was charged, we walked across town to a nearby school. It was open as a shelter for those immediately affected by the catastrophe. As you'd expect people to act during times like this, Neanderthals scoured the streets at sunset. In the night, they looted stores and wreaking havoc on nearby businesses and homes. The city was bought down to its knees. This caused the police to be on high alert.

We followed the line of people inside the school. A few police officers stood at the door as guards. My mom tried to ask one of the officers on site about the city's status, but she was shooed away like a fly, to her surprise. Appalled, she yelled at the man, who was now just as frustrated as she.

"Ma'am," he screamed at her as he reached for the 9-millimeter pistol on his hip. "You need to get in the auditorium and sit down!" My mother continued to scream. I stood between her and the officer, attempting to push her back.

"Woman, stand down!" the cop said one more time as he drew his gun and pointed at her. Scared, I stared at the officer. He locked eyes with her as his hand shook, finger in the trigger well of the gun.

"Dr. Simms!" a woman came from the door and tugged the two of us. The officer put his gun back in his holster and walked away, leaving the other officers to handle the citizens.

We entered the auditorium full of people in various forms of disarray. The woman walked us to one side of the room, where there was a bit of open space for seating.

"Dr. Simms.", the woman called out to my mom, but she

was in shock and did not say a word. She stared off into space with a blank expression on her face. She made absolutely no movement after sitting down in the chair. I grabbed her hand, and immediately she grappled my fingers and squeezed. In pain, I screamed for her, which snapped her out of the trance. She looked down at me and pulled me close to her, and finally noticed the woman that brought us in here.

"Abbie!?" my mom called out to the woman who stepped forward and hugged her.

"What are you doing here? I thought you went back to Virginia."

"I was heading out of the city when the quake happened." The young blond woman with dark brown eyes answered. "I am so happy to see you!"

"Apparently, there is absolutely no contact to anywhere else outside of the state. We are quarantined for some reason."

"Quarantined? Why?"

"Mommy, what is quarter team?" I innocently asked.

"Milo, hold on, sweetie." The young woman looked around for a moment, careful not to stir up trouble.

"I don't want to alarm you, but I think it may have something to do with the research you have been doing."

Mom looked like she had become ill. She even held on to her stomach and leaned forward into her own lap, and began to take deep breaths.

"Dr. Simms, it will be okay." The woman said.

"Milo, say hi to Ms. Calloway." she directed me. I stepped over to the woman and extended my right hand like a gentleman with a massive smile on my face. She took my hand and shook it firmly with a smile to match. My mother took the opportunity to calm herself down.

The Gem State Siege

"You can call me, Ms. Abbie. And you are?" she asked.
"I'm Milo."
"Such a gentleman. It is a pleasure meeting you, Milo."
"The pleasure is all mine," I said as I kissed the back of her hand. It was something that I had recently seen in a movie that I watched with my mom and dad.
"It is so hard to believe that he is only five years old." She said.
"I'll be six next month."
"Will you?" she laughed. "You'll almost be an adult."
I smiled at her and began to fidget with my hands.

"Abbie, what do you know?" my mom asked her.
"Remember that relic thing that you researched a few years back? Well, apparently, there have been experiments taking place on it. Supposedly, it caused a lot of people to get infected." She said as she continued to look around for listening ears. "Rumor has it that they blew up the 15 as an excuse to lock down the city. By this time tomorrow, they'll be locking down the entire state."
"Why?"
"They claim that people in this state and any that borders it are likely to mutate into something dangerous. So their only option is to kill everyone."
"Is it the government?"
"I honestly don't know."
"Mommy, what happened?" I asked.
"Nothing, sweetie. Everything is fine."
"Where is Mr. Simms?" Abbie asked.
"He's doing research somewhere in Yellowstone and isn't scheduled to return until next week."

The woman turned forward and began to think.

"Do you think they realized that he is from here and locked him down?" asked Abbie.

"I hope not."

"I hope this is all just precaution of the gaping hole in the highway, and we are overthinking it."

"I don't know, Abbie," my mother said as she tilted her head back to stare at the ceiling with worry. "If this is the thing that we've been researching, then we don't really stand a chance."

CHAPTER V

One-hundred miles northeast, my father sat in a lab placed in a secret location near Yellowstone National Park. He had been there with little to no sleep for days, working on a string of research that he conducted for his boss. His colleagues remained diligent, despite not knowing why their jobs were important. Usually, he would not complain about the mess that was his job. But, he was getting an earful from my mom, and the pressure was getting to him. The new obstacle was about 5' 4", 127 pounds, and long black hair—a woman who is always timid and usually a bit of a bookworm. Who seemed to have been breaking out of her shell.

So there he was, sitting in this small, dark office with two, side-by-side, L-shaped tables in it. His desk surface hidden under seismographs and a device known as a kaitron observer. This was a gadget that measured energy from living organisms. His task was to evaluate the energy that radiated from underneath the geysers that sat all over the park.

"Hey Simms, you okay over there?" another scientist asked my dad, seeing the blank stare on his face.

"Yup. I was just thinking of something my wife told me earlier."

"Yeah, what's that?"

"She is not happy about the extra-long sabbatical from our marriage." The man looked over his computer monitor at my dad and gave his full attention with an eyebrow raised.

"You tell her how important your job is, right?"

"No, because I don't disagree with her."

"What do you mean? Everything we do here keeps people like your wife able to live their jolly, care-free lives."

"I guess I shouldn't tell you about the suspicious activity

that I found. You know... researching Project Pyro Stone, huh."

The man then reacted with total disbelief as he found my dad's words inconceivable.
"Simms!" he called out.
"What exactly are you referring to?"
My dad's suspicion only grew as he looked at the man in wonder. He thought about all the conspiracies in the world that my mom introduced him to. He back-peddled the conversation and got quiet.
"Now, I'm curious." the other scientist said.
"Yeah, me too," my dad said while standing from his chair.
"Answer me this," he said.
"What exactly do you know about our boss? Or what this company needs all this research for? None of this seems odd to you?" The man tilted his head and started up to the corner of the room.
"Simms, this company paid for my wife and me to go to school. Why would I not trust their process?" My father stared at him before taking a deep breath.
"You have fun in here. I'm going to get something to eat, finally."
"Hey, Simms." He called out before my dad left the room. He turned to look at the man."Stay under the radar, will ya?"
"I'll do my best."
My father walked out into the hall and immediately pulled out his phone to call my mom. But as the call connected, he immediately reached her voice mail. Patiently, he waited for her to finish, then the beep.
"Hey Tawnie, I just want you to know something.—" My dad said his peace, hung up the phone, leaned against the

wall, and took a deep breath. He had no idea what was truly happening on our side. Nor did he expect what was about to happen to him. He went back into the office after his break and took a seat at his desk. With the other guy out of the room, he decided to dig a little deeper. He hoped he could find something to help him understand the mission.

It wasn't enough to do all these sideline projects to no end if they were adversely affecting his marriage. My dad had a hunger and needed to know what it was that he was supporting. That is when he found it. He clicked through the file system and found an encrypted folder labeled Phase."
"What is this?" he asked himself as he clicked on the file. When the credentials screen popped up, he closed it in suspicion that it could be tracked. A camera in the top corner of the room looked right in his direction. The angle peeked over his shoulder and in the direction of his office mate. Curious about the file, he stepped over to the door to see if anyone was out there.

My dad pulled out his phone and noticed that he had no notifications from anything. My mom had not called him back. The flood of texts that he usually gets around 4pm and all his calls had somehow stopped. For experiment, he looked into his connection section on the phone's menu. He was astonished. Something external was giving his phone the illusion that he still had service. But upon closer inspection, he realized that he had no data connection. Another operating system was mirroring his phone system. He tried turning off the Wi-Fi signal to see if it made a difference, but that was to no avail. The only thing that made a difference was placing the phone on airplane mode. He went back into the office and sat at his office mate's computer. His screen did not have a

The Gem State Siege

direct line of sight to the camera above.

He hurried to find the same encrypted folder on the company's shared drive and attempted to access it. He began to run a script that allowed him to crack the password of the folder. He skipped past the Phase II and went to the Phase I file. He opened it and saw the footage from the incident on the I-15. Shocked, he began to worry about my mom and me.

He thought about the last words he said to mom as she was stuck on the I-15. He wondered if this was the reason that the call was lost. Suddenly, he heard footsteps coming down the long hallway. He panicked as he shuffled around for something quick to implement at the moment. He grabbed a flash drive from his pocket, plugged it into the computer, and moved the files over. When the other scientist walked into the room, my father sitting at his own computer. He was looking at his phone with concern on his face as he had an eyebrow raised.

"You good, Simms?" the other man asked.

"I don't know, man," he responded. "Is your phone actually working?"

"What do you mean?" he asked as the man sat down at his desk.

"I just can't seem to do anything. I'll take it to the carrier and let them handle it."

"Could just need a reset."

"Yeah, maybe."

"Hey, what is the hourly report at right now?" he asked my father.

"Seismographs are showing little to no activity at the moment. But the energy detector is picking up a massive amount of energy underneath the surface of the park."

"How much?"

"Kaitron count is around 30 million."

"30 million?!" he responded as he began to write in an open notebook on the desk.

"Hey, what do you think that thing is anyway?"

"Some say a gift from the heavens. I think it is forgotten technology from our ancestors. The forefathers of this world."

The strange scientist turned around and leaned over to reach a lower cabinet on his desk. My father took the opportunity to unplug the flash drive from the back of his computer. Upon hearing my father jump up from his seat, the other man quickly turned to him in suspicion.

"You okay?" he asked my dad.

"Yeah, just readjusting." The man stared at him as if he wanted to say something." It's about the end of my shift, so I am going to head out." He said to the strange scientist.

"Alright then. See you tomorrow." He responded. My father got himself situated and made his way out of the room. The strange scientist watched him closely as he left.

CHAPTER VI

My dad hurried out of the research facility and tried his best not to talk to anyone on his way. Once he exited the building, he looked at his phone again to see if anything had changed but, no luck. He tried to send a call to my mom again, and he watched the data icons as the lines appeared to connect. He thought he was paranoid. My mom's voice mail started to play. He made the call seem real as to not tip anyone off that he was on to them. He left a voice message on her phone and hung up as usual. Because he knew that the cameras were on him, he played it safe and didn't do anything he wouldn't normally do. He left the facility and headed back to the lodging area they provided him.

My dad worked for this company for years, and he always had issues with how they operated. Lured in by false promises and goals that seemed to line up with his personal mission. He wanted to focus on uncovering resources to help mankind progress. But after acquiring him as an asset, he was forced to do things he did not support. This company is a tech-based giant known as Primotech. So it led to the question, what are they trying to cover up and why? A tech-conglomerate digging in the woods didn't make any sense.

My father got back to his quarters, opened his computer, placed the flash drive in the USB port. He wasted no time opening the files to scan through the contents. Amazed at what he had stumbled across, he became worried. Hundreds of folders filled with pictures and documents of the company's assets. The problem was not the fact that the company owned these assets but the nature and how they

The Gem State Siege

would get them.

I could talk to you forever, it seems, about the shady doings of this organization, but this story is only about one. To knock down the first domino of calamity, Primotech discovered the whereabouts of a relic. Now, I know what you may think, a relic? Big deal! But this is no figurine or antique that you'd find at a beach shop.

My father thought of it as insane. Fire-bending, water bending humans? The thought was inconceivable. But, here is research from a group of scientists who thought it possible. Primotech was getting massive payouts from organizations worldwide fund the experiments.

    He stumbled across video footage of an incident caused by kaitron radiation from the Pyro Stone. The time stamp on the file showed that it was from earlier that day, and immediately his heart sank. As he clicked on the video, he could see Idaho Falls from an aerial view on what appeared to be a typical day. But, something wasn't right. A heads-up display showed excessive amounts of energy all over the city. The energy that bled from the ground caused a heatwave that turned this winter day into a summer scorcher.

My dad started to link the two ideas and realized, this was his own doing. The display on the video showed a drastic change in energy to the west. But, one random spot in the city had a reading of two-million kaitrons and climbing. This was the area around the highway.

In the video, he noticed the land somehow moving. The flat ground lifted and fell as if the Earth was breathing. We didn't even see it in the traffic jam, but he watched the video of what happened at 2× speed.

"How?" he asked himself at the moment. He had seen some strange phenomenon in his profession but never on this scale. Suddenly, like a geyser in Yellowstone, a spout of flames shot up from the highway and cut off traffic. The time stamp on the video now showed 2:18, and at this point, my mom was calling him.

At 2:26pm, the time that the call dropped, it happened.

But this event that merely looked like an earthquake from the ground seemed different from the sky. A symmetrical ring of fire shot up from the ground, enclosing part of the highway. A giant ball of flames shot up from the center, followed by a collapse of the land inside the ring.

My dad scurried for a sheet of paper and a pen so he could draw out what he saw. As a finale, the flames created a symbol that warned us all of what was to become. Being in the middle of the chaos was scary in itself. I saw this video many times during my life. I could say, knowing what the symbol means now, that it is much more terrifying. He turned off the video and contemplated the worst. As he removed his glasses, he wiped the sweat from his forehead. He closed his laptop and tried to piece together his thoughts. Connecting dots that belonged to the company that now had control over his life.

He had to face the reality that his wife's conspiracies about powered people were real. The evidence was in front of him. Pictures and videos of people doing things that humans were not supposed to. She has even constructed her brand to be the go-to authority of exposing the world's conspiracies. My father tried his best to create a barrier of normalcy in his own

The Gem State Siege

world. But that shield broke away that day.

I have to say that it gets worse from here. Unfortunately, none of us was safe. Even I was a target now. My father took a hard swallow as he realized what he had done. He got up from his desk and looked down at the laptop and flash drive. Trouble was brewing, and he winced at the thought of the trouble that he was in.

"Boom, boom, boom," he heard at the front door. My father stood there in the living room watching the door, trying to develop a plan on the spot. But he knew that this was about to be the end.

CHAPTER VII

"Who is it?" my dad asked in response to the knock on the door. As he waited for an answer, he scurried for his belongings in case he needed to make a run for it.

"Boom, boom, boom, boom!" the knocks got louder. At this point, his heart pounded from his chest. He walked over to the door and put his bag next to it to seem less suspicious when he opened it. After seeing that the peephole on the door was being covered, his body quivered in fear.

He began to look around to create an exit strategy. But they had to know he was there because he had already spoken. He had no choice but to open the door and face whoever stood on the other side. His hand, trembling with fear, reached down and grabbed the doorknob. He took a deep breath and closed his eyes as a small prayer passed from his lips in a desperate whisper.

As he opened the door, he noticed three large men that appeared to be a part of some military task force. The men in black combat gear. One even had a rifle strapped to his back.

"Gentlemen?" he said to them after they stared at him for a moment.

"You need to come with us." the man in the front said to him.

"Why?" he asked. Instead of answering, the man repeated himself. The other two men grabbed him by his arm and dragged him down the hall.

"Guys, what is this about?" he asked again.

Minutes later, my dad found himself sitting in a small room with a small square table and two chairs. The big men sat him down at the table and stood there waiting with their arms crossed. He waited a few moments to determine what the men were doing. A quick look around, and my dad would see a lot of peculiar items in the room. There were knives and bolt cutters of all sizes on one of the walls. Large tiles lined one corner in particular with a large drain on the floor. The room reeked of an unexplainable odor that had him sick to his stomach.

After a few minutes of waiting, the door opened. Into the room stepped a clean shaved man with slicked back, black hair, and a tailored suit. The young gentleman sat across the tiny table. My dad watched him the entire time as he reached up and undid his necktie. He caught a glimpse of his shiny gold watch and knew that this guy was of high status.

"Mr. Simms." the young man said with a slight grin. Dad stayed quiet as he kept eye contact with the man.
"You may have something that belongs to me." the man said.
"I'm sorry?" he responded. "Who are you again?"
"How insulting."
"I don't think we've met, Mister..."
"Maxwell."
"Maxwell?" My dad said as he began to cringe. "As in..."
"Jacob Maxwell, your boss."
"Mr. Maxwell, I assure you that I don't have anything of yours."
"Hmm. Right." Maxwell responded as he leaned back in the chair. "Before we go into this game of chicken, Mr. Simms, know that I am not a man big on patience."
"I can imagine, Mr. Maxwell. But, I am in no position to lie to you."

The Gem State Siege

The two men glared at one another. But to seem less intimidating, my father shifted his eyes to the surface of the table. Maxwell waved over one of the guards, who handed him a manila folder.

"Is there anything you would like to tell me before we proceed, Mr. Simms?"

"No, continue, Mr. Maxwell."

Maxwell slid his hand into the folder and pulled out a hi-def photo of my father. It was the moment he put a flash drive into his officemate's computer. Shocked, my father's eyes popped as he turned the picture, then slid it across the table. Maxwell smiled in a last attempt to be polite.

"I need to know, Mr. Simms, why exactly would one of my staff be so sneaky with a simple flash drive?"

"Mr. Maxwell, I can assure you—"

"SILENCE!" Maxwell snarled at him. "You may want to produce that flash drive right now if you know what's good for you." At that moment, the men behind my father began to crack their knuckles.

One of the guards threw my dad's belongings on the table and stepped back. He looked around at them, and Maxwell urged him to hurry it along. Hesitantly, he unzipped the backpack. My dad found the flash drive and gave it over to Maxwell. One of the grunts handed him a computer, and he did not skip a beat to plug it in. My father raised an eyebrow as he watched the rich playboy search through the contents of the device.

"What the hell is this?" he asked.

"Excuse me?" my dad responded.

The Gem State Siege

"Why were you seen on camera planting this drive on your office mate's computer?" Maxwell asked.

"To give that weirdo a virus."

"A virus? Why?"

"With all due respect, sir, have you met him?"

"Hmph. There must be another drive. Shake him down! Now!"

The three men stood him up and threw him against the wall, patting down every inch of his body. One guard even dumping everything out of my dad's backpack all over the dirty floor. Even his laptop fell from the bag and bounced on the concrete.

"No!" he screamed as he went to get his laptop, attempting to break away from the thugs. But they took the opportunity to pin him against the wall to finish their search.

"Nothing, boss." one thug said to Maxwell.

Maxwell sat there scratching his head for a moment and stared at my father.

"What was really on the flash drive?" he asked again.

"A Trojan horse virus that slowed down that weirdo's computer."

"Anyone confirm that?" Suddenly, a woman opens the door and peaks into the room to answer.

"The computer has a virus, sir." She said.

"Interesting," Maxwell replied. "Did you really just risk your freedom for a crude joke?"

"Had I known, this would have been sidelined."

"If you're lying, I will find out." He said as his voice dropped an octave or two.

"So, am I free to go?" My dad asked him. Maxwell

placed his hand on his chin and glared at him.

"Yeah, you are most certainly free." He answered. "But don't ever come back."

"Wait!" my dad said in shock.

"You're fired."

Jacob Maxwell jumped up from his seat and pulled on his collar to fix it.

"You got lucky, Mr. Simms. This could have gone a lot worse." The three guards left the room, and Maxwell followed them out. My father was not a confrontational man, so he did not cause a scene. This situation could have gone a lot worse, and he could have lost a lot more. My father walked out of there alive. But he was determined to get the actual flash drive back home.

CHAPTER VIII

My dad began to leave the Yellowstone facility but struggled to find a way home. He was brought there by company vehicles that carpooled a lot of staff members to the site. Jacob Maxwell made sure that he was on his own. As my old man walked away from the site, he noticed a lot of activity behind the building they were stationed. It was at this moment dad decided not to be so passive about his life. He figured that if something was going on, then he should spread the word. He examined the environment. He could hear a machine of some sort behind the facility and see lights shining. Without fear, he followed his senses. When he arrived at the light source, he noticed many construction lights pointing to a random spot in the grass. Confused, he stared at a concrete walkway that seemed to stop in the middle of the field. Suddenly, he heard a loud mechanical sound. A large patch of grass lifted from the earth to reveal a tunnel. Two soldiers exited a hatch and walked to the main building, yards away. My dad hid behind a stack of crates at the edge of the property and waited. Seconds later, the hatch closed.

He had a pit in his stomach, knowing that he would not be able to live with himself if he did not get the truth. Once the hatch slammed shut, he knew that it would be a challenge to get in. One more soldier came out of the main building. As he approached, a keypad protruded from the ground. He scanned his ID Badge, and the hatch lifted again. He noticed a duct of some sort that went into the ground within a few feet of the hatch. He took a moment to recognize the dangers involved with trying to get inside. He knew that these men were ready to shoot and attack anything on sight.

My dad found an access hatch to the ductwork and slipped inside. The cables and tubes that the duct was hiding were massive. As he shimmied under the surface, he noticed a pair of guards inside the opening. They stood at a flight of steps guarding the entrance. The two men were having a conversation as my dad managed to crawl inside.

"I'm not used to having the boss around." One man said to another.
"Yeah, it definitely feels more hostile whenever he arrives, doesn't it?" Said the other.
"He's always killing people."
"Come on, Tyson, you're a trained killer. Don't tell me that you have a problem with doing your job."
"No, but this is all dangerous, man." The guard pleaded. "But, what if Primotech found out about all of this?"
"Then knowing the boss, we would be going to war with them too."

Completely interrupting the conversation, my dad stumbled against the sheet metal. One guard cut off the other.
"Shh shh shh!" He looked around.
"What is it?" The other asked.
"I don't know. Did you hear that?"
"I didn't hear anything. You getting paranoid again?"
"No, I heard something!"
"It was probably another mouse or a rabbit or something. Calm down."

My dad was careful that he didn't move, cautious not to make any more noise and raise further suspicion. But as he looked around the access duct, he noticed a hatch above him and a valve and control box behind him. He hurried past the hatch. As his toes moved past the opening, the thug opened the hatch. But, my dad had already squeezed through.

"You gonna chill out now, man?" The other guard asked the paranoid one.
"I know I heard something." He said.
"Maybe you did. But if someone else was here, we'd know it."
"Yeah, I guess you're right."
The two men laughed as my dad made his way through the narrow shaft.

As he got deeper inside the tunnel, it had gotten hot, and he could not stand to be in the duct any longer. He crawled through until he reached another hatch. He opened it to look out at his surroundings and saw no one. After determining that the coast was clear, he jumped out of the duct and quietly closed it.

He headed deeper inside the tunnel and noticed that the heat was getting more intense with each step. He thought that he was getting delirious as he began to see heat waves all around him. He headed deeper inside the tunnel and followed the ductwork. The tunnel came to its end, and my dad noticed a machine. Tubes, cables, and hoses all extruded the device as if it was a generator of some sort.

He took a moment to examine the machine. It was like nothing that he'd ever seen before. It appeared to be futuristic. The machine had a window on the front with an object inside that glowed. Mesmerized, he stared at the window as the item dazzled with a red light.

With immense caution, he opened the compartment and immediately recognized the glowing object. The object was like a glass orb that housed a flame on the inside. My dad had seen this object in his research. This object was just a legend at some point, but now it was at my dad's fingertips. He began to realize that the machine in front of him was a kaitron extractor.

He stood in front of the extractor for a moment and weighed out his options. Grabbing the object would only set off alarms and cause him to be the target of what seemed to be an entire military. If he left it there, there is no telling what would happen to the world. My dad reached forward, wrapped his hands around the orb, and pulled it out of the extractor. This was how the calamity began, this moment right here. The moment that man touched the relic created by the gods; The Pyro Orb.

CHAPTER IX

Back in Idaho Falls, my mom and I sat among her friend, Abbie, and other citizens affected by the catastrophe.

"Where do you think it will go from here?" One woman asked.

"God will bring us out through the other side, my dear." An elderly woman said in response. "There is nothing on Earth able to stop the will of God. He will put an end to all these meta-human mumbo jumbo and everyone greedy for power!"

"Ma'am?" My mother called out to the woman. The elder looked locked eyes with her. She then looked down at me as I gripped my mother's arms.

"You don't have faith, child?" The woman asked.

"I do, but I am no fan of religion, and that's not how I want to teach my son. So if you don't mind." She told the woman.

"Dr. Simms?" Abbie called out to her.

"Doctor?" the elderly woman asked with a hint of attitude. "I should have known that."

"Ma'am, I was simply asking if you could refrain from talking like that around my son."

"If he has a mother like you, then I'm not sure that I can."

"Ma'am, can you let it go?" Abbie asked.

"I can't let go of the word of God, child. Just because your friend here is a doctor, she feels like she is above all religion. God don't care about the fact that you know science, sweetheart."

"That's a good guess, but I'm actually Ph.D., not MD."

"Mm." The woman said as she began to sway from side to

side in her seat. The tension stayed around for a moment, even though the conversation was over.

My mom stood up from the chair, took a deep breath, and handed me off to Abbie.
"Can you keep him while I go to the restroom?" Abbie held me close and sent my mom off. She and the old woman still held eye contact as she walked away.

When she arrived, there was a small line leading to the women's restroom. As she stood waiting, her attention was outside the window. In the distance, she could see black SUVs rolling through the city. As she watched the commotion outside, the line vanished. She got inside and entered a stall. In the process, she noticed sniffling in the stall next to her. She tried to ignore it, thinking that it was a woman crying about the disaster. She prepared to get up and walk away, but she couldn't leave her there, sobbing.

As she was about to ask the woman a question, she noticed something strange. There was a strange glow on the floor and the ceiling of the next stall. Seconds after the light ignited, the woman screeched in agonizing pain.
"Excuse me? Are you okay?" Mom asked. But she received no answer, and the crying continued.
My mom finished up in the stall and stepped out of it. Other women who were in the restroom had all walked out in fear. My mom saw the door closing behind the last person to leave. She went to knock on the stall door and ask again if everything was okay. But once again, the woman did not answer.

"Ma'am, should I go get someone?" She asked. Finally,

the woman yelled, "Leave me alone!"

Shocked, my mom flinched as she noticed sparks of light coming from inside.

"I understand." She said to the woman. "This could all be scary if you do this alone. Do you have any family here?"

"I can't!" The woman yelled.

"Why? Do you not want their help?"

"I don't want them to see me like this!" she cried out.

"Hey, your powers are beautiful, don't be afraid of them."

"But, I can't control them."

"And that's okay, as long as you're trying, everything will be okay." My mom talked to that woman in that bathroom for about twenty minutes to get her to calm down. That woman's story will cross ours soon, but not now.

As my mom walked out of the restroom, she looked out of the window she passed before. It seemed like the number of black SUVs had multiplied. She assumed that they were here for aid and relief. But she could not tell who the organization was.

She looked around at the people inside the building, wondering if anyone saw the same thing. But it seemed as if nobody actually cared about what was happening. Unfortunately, my mom knew this maneuver well. The pattern in which the vehicles sat outside were roadblocks. Brave yet foolish, my mom took the opportunity to exit the school and inquire about the siege.

She approached one of the vehicles at the corner by the school. Two men were standing in front of a bulletproof SUV wearing all black. They were the same group that my dad was currently dealing with in the Northeast.

"Excuse me, what is all of this?" She asked the men.

"A routine check." One of the men responded.

"For?"

"In the event of a natural disaster, it is our job to maintain peace."

"Oh, what are you here to do?"

"We make sure that nobody gets hurt during times like these."

"Right." She said with suspicion.

"If you don't mind ma'am, we would like to get you to explain what happened so we can have a report on file." The man requested of her. She looked around. She then saw others following the soldiers to their base of operation.

"Okay." She agreed. The two men walked her over to a large tent, like the medical outpost she was in earlier. There were many people in the tent sitting across from representatives of this group.

"Alright, go sit at an open table, and we will get started." The man said as he began to leave.

"Wait. Get started with what?" She asked. Ignoring her, the men walked away. Being the rebel she is, my mom stood along the side of the tent, being sure to stay out of the way. She paid close attention to the environment. It felt uneasy about the entire situation. She watched how the people in the tent moved. Many hand gestures and symbols were passed among them. This made her think twice about what was going on behind the scenes.

"Ma'am, would you like to give us a statement?" A man asked her. Still looking around at her environment, my mom shook her head.

"I actually think I'm going to go." She said to him. As she walked past the man, he put his arm up to block the exit.

"You should stay for a moment." He continued, a little

more serious than before. She looked down at his other hand and noticed that it was on his gun. Her heart dropped as she stepped backward, eyes locked into his cold stare.

That is when she noticed that people were being escorted to a section in the back. An opening too dark to be an exit.

"What are you here for?" She asked him.

"We are just doing the work of science." He answered. "I think it's your time to go through the curtain, Mrs. Simms."

"What? How do you know my name?" She asked.

"You will be a martyr, but that is the price that we pay for perfection and obscurity."

"What are you talking about?"

The man shoved my mother towards the back of the tent through the dark exit. She saw the curtain flip for a second and noticed that the opening led into another tent. It was well lit with blood-splattered plastic everywhere. There, the face of an innocent woman looked at her, taking her last breath. Immediately, my mother flailed as she was reluctant to enter the slaughter room. Suddenly, a man yelled into the tent from the front entrance.

"Run, it's happening again!" He screamed. My mother turned towards the entrance and saw the officer that she argued with inside the school. Everyone inside the tent screamed as they all tried to exit at the same time in fear. My mom took the opportunity to flee. She locked eyes with the police officer as they both ran towards the school.

She ran in a full sprint. Police officers at the door stopped her to figure out why she was so frantic.

"We need to get these people out of the school!" She yelled. The officers ignored her and opened the door for her to go in with grins on their faces. She entered the school on a

The Gem State Siege

mission as she heard the sound of gunshots in the distance.

CHAPTER X

Things had escalated outside of the school. She immediately found Abbie and me in the spot where she left us. The old woman nearby spent a few moments complaining about how powered people. Tired of hearing it, I was happy to finally see my mom again.

"Dr. Simms?" Abbie called out.

"Abbie, we have to go!" she said as she pulled me up by the arm. Abbie jumped up from her seat with great concern.

"Dr. Simms, what happened?" She asked.

"I'll explain later!" My mom said to her as she pushed the girl through the crowd.

As we made our way down the hall, we heard a loud crash from behind. The two women stopped and looked back to see what happened. That is when the militant group burst through the doors with guns drawn and armor on.

"Go, go!" Mom yelled at Abbie.

The two of them ran through the school, attempting to break through the crowd. Everyone crowded the one door that seemed to be safe and packed the hall.

"Mom!" I screamed, becoming afraid of the commotion around us. She was being shoved around as the crowd grew rowdy.

"Dr. Simms!" Abbie yelled as we were separated from us. The crowd slowly made it out of the door to what seemed like safety. But the group flanked the back of the building and began to spray bullets into the door. The screams of the people masked the guns' sound, but my mom knew what was happening. As she tried to run in the opposite direction, people still pushed against her trying to get outside. When

The Gem State Siege

she finally broke through, we ran through the halls to find somewhere to hide. As she tried to open doors down the hall, she realized that all of them were locked. She ran past a locker in the empty hall and saw that it was open with a broken lock. Mom ran over to the locker and told me to step inside. She kneeled in front of me and looked around for a moment.

"Milo, we are going to play a little game, okay?" She said to me. Tears running down my face, I nodded my head.

"Mommy is going to leave you here to hide from the bad men. But you have to be absolutely quiet, so they don't find you, okay?" She asked again. At this point, I cried even more as I begged her to stay with me. Not realizing what I was asking her to do. This was when I started to understand how much of a chess player and master strategist she actually was.

She closed the locker and ran down the hall. Immediately, I heard gunshots. At that moment, I went dead silent and remained still. When the bullets stopped flying, the men flanked the hall. They looked into the classrooms for survivors as they swept through. There was a small vent at the bottom of the locker door that I could see out to the floor. The men stepped in front of the locker, and I could see their feet. I wished that there was something that I could do at that moment other than wring my hands together. But what could a five-year-old do to stop a tyrannical military force?

"Did we get them all?" One of the soldiers asked.
"I don't think so." Said another.
"Okay. Let's sweep back out."

After what felt like minutes, the men walked away from the locker, and I was finally able to breathe again. But, I was too afraid to move. On the other side of the building, my mother had a risky plan that she implemented after noticing that she was the only survivor. As she ran towards the door surrounded by hundreds of dead bodies, she was careful to make sure that she was followed. She jumped on top of the bodies and headed towards the door. The men had finally stepped into the hall. My mother reached down and clenched her fist in blood, and stood back up. She then waited for the soldier to shoot. She screeched, and I could hear her from the locker and immediately sobbed. But, my mother fell to the ground, staring at the ceiling. She gargled on blood as she took her last breath. The men approached her and pointed their guns at her, but the deed was done.

"Next phase." One of the soldiers said to the others. They all stepped over the bodies as if they were hiking on rough terrain.

Minutes later, they brought gas cans inside the building. They also dragged the bodies of the people they exterminated outside. Soldiers poured the gas out in the halls of the building, preparing it to be set ablaze.

"How do you think they will cover this one up?" One soldier asked.

"They'll say some goofy shit on the news, like, hundreds of people of Idaho Falls gathered at this school to mourn the people lost in the catastrophe..."

"When a rogue cigarette set the building on fire with all the people inside."

All the men laughed at the joke and continued working. I remember them coming past the locker that I was in and splashing gasoline on it. This stifled the air inside, and it began to choke me. I knew that if I opened the locker, I would have to face the men, but I would die regardless. I began to hear the men leaving after a few minutes of talking in the hall. Once they left, I tried to push the locker door open, but I didn't have the strength to do so after going so long with no oxygen. The building was getting dark in the setting sun, but the flames grew brighter as they engulfed the halls. The fire reached the locker door, and at this point, I was about to blackout due to smoke inhalation. Suddenly, the locker door swung open, and in flames and black smoke stood the police officer from the door. He hurried to grab me, put me over his shoulder, and ran through the school. I passed out as he searched around for a way through the flames.

I am unsure how he got us out, but I woke up on the ground outside with my mother giving me CPR to bring me back to life. Once I opened my eyes, I felt dizzy, and I saw triple. My mom held on to me, crying tears of joy. She kissed me on my cheek and forehead a few times, and the police officer reminded us that we needed to leave. I noticed that he had a large gun in his hands that he had taken from a soldier. His body was bruised and beaten with blood on his uniform as if he was shot a few times.

"Okay, let's get out of here." She said to us and pulled me up from the ground.

"Where do you need to go?" He asked her.

"I need to go Northeast." She said. "I can go home and get a car."

"Do you mind if I come."

"Officer, you saved me. Of course, you can come with us. I actually insist."

"Gordon."

"Huh?" My mom asked as she did not hear what he said.

"The name is Gordon." He expanded.

"Mr. Gordon, I'm Tawnie Simms, and this is my son,

Milo." She said with a smile and a blush.

"Well, it is nice to meet you. Both of you."

"Is there no backup coming?" My mom asked.

"I'm afraid not. It seems that this group, whoever they are, has eliminated everyone in Idaho Falls. If we don't leave now, we're next."

CHAPTER XI

Exiting the city felt like it took forever. Once we left the school, we noticed soldiers everywhere. Blockades closed the roads, and vehicles were on patrol all over. I remember thinking this was the scariest thing, and I remember that day well. I remember watching something break in my mom for the second time in just a few days. It was like a metamorphosis the world was not prepared for. We skated through the city, trying to be as inconspicuous as possible. We were heading to the outskirts of Idaho Falls. Once we reached the city's limits, mom looked back at the burning skyline with eyes full of tears. Many buildings burned with the remains of the citizens who were slaughtered that day. Idaho Falls was up in flames of injustice would burn with nobody alive to extinguish them. Officer Gordon placed his hand on my mom's shoulder as she sobbed. She fell to her knees, and I wrapped my arms around her, hoping to relieve some of the pain. But the darkness was setting in on her spirit. As she mourned, Officer Gordon urged us to keep moving.

Officer Gordon led the way through the fields, away from the roads. My mom told him where we lived, and he did his best to assure that we didn't get spotted on our journey.
"Mommy, when are we getting home." I asked as I stopped walking in the grass.
"We're almost there, sweetie, but we have to keep moving, okay?" She answered.
"Where is daddy?" She looked forward as she pulled me along. Just before I asked again, she glared at me.

"Milo, how old are you?" Officer Gordon asked to cut the tension.

"I'm five." I answered.

"Oh wow!" He said as he looked back at me. "You are a pretty big five-year-old. Have you been eating your veggies?"

"Yes, sir."

"I bet you will grow into a fine young man. And I'm sure you will always take care of your mother, correct?"

"Yes!" I responded as I stepped out in front of my mom with my arms up, pretending to be tough.

The large muscular man laughed as he kept walking. It had gotten quiet for a moment as we approached our neighborhood.

"You are pretty good with kids." My mom said to him.

"Is that leading to a question?" He asked her.

"Do you have any... kids, I mean."

"No, I just have the experience." It got quiet again, and the mood became awkward between them.

"So, how did you get away?"

"Do we have to talk about that now?"

"Either that or why you pointed your gun at me earlier."

The man turned around to look at my mom, and she stopped in front of him.

"You make it a habit of pointing guns at innocent women and children?" she asked him.

"I don't have to answer that."

"Is it because I'm black?" She asked.

"You think that it was an act of racism? Why am I not surprised?"

"What does that even mean?"

"You people always look at us as the problem whenever you have disagreements with 'The Man,'" he said. Shocked, my mother stood there as he turned to keep walking.

"You people?!" She screamed. "You people?! You mean monkeys, Negroes, slaves?"

"Would you stop it already!?" He turned and yelled at her. "That was not about you, now let it go! Please."

The two of them stared at one another and remained quiet for a moment as animosity built between them. We continued and walked a little further in the fields, and my mom stopped for a moment.

"What is it?" Gordon asked.

"Helicopters." My mom answered as she listened to her environment.

"Shit, seriously?"

"They're close."

"They're probably in the neighborhood and patrolling it for survivors here too." Gordon said as he stepped forward, signaling my mom and me to stop.

"What the hell are you doing?" She asked him with concern in her voice.

"Don't seem so worried about me." He said as he walked backward. "I'll lead them away from you and Milo while you two make your way to your house. That ought to buy you some time."

"And that would be what we call a bad plan." she said as she followed him.

"You will get you and your son killed."

"He will be fine! But I need all the help I can get." She said as she walked past him. "Even if you are a racist bastard. I can't let you sacrifice yourself for me."

Officer Gordon began to shake his head as he slowly

walked behind us.

As we reached the neighborhood, we could hear the helicopters like they were overhead.

"Dammit!" Gordon yelled. "We have to hide."

"Where?" My mom asked as she waved around to the open field around us.

Gordon saw the helicopter with a spotlight shining down into the neighborhood. It flew low as it floated over the yards and began to swing around and head in our direction. In front of us was the wooden fence that surrounded the neighborhood. On the opposite side of that stood a house. Gordon jumped up to the top of the fence and noticed a place that could serve as quick cover. He came back down and told us what he saw as he grabbed my mom and sent her up the face of the fence.

"Mommy!" I yelled as Gordon threw me over the fence like a doll. She caught me and ran toward the house. Gordon jumped the wall behind us. My mom and I ran over to a wooden rear deck of the house. We found a small opening in the lattice surrounding it and crawled underneath. As the helicopter peeked over the house, the spotlight rose over the yard like the sunrise. The light was heading right towards Gordon. My mom placed her hand over her mouth as she gasped in fear that he would get spotted. He had no time to run to the deck but in the center of the yard sat a picnic table. In anticipation of how he would get out of this, she began to panic. As the spotlight hit the picnic table, Gordon slid across the grass and hid underneath.

My mother sighed a breath of relief, excited that he made it. Suddenly, we realized something was wrong. The helicopter stopped, and the spotlight stopped moving directly on the table. My mom looked horrified as she made eye contact with Gordon. He made a face suggesting that he wanted to make a run for it. But she held a finger up and shook her head. He was stranded. Gordon was about to do something illogical when the helicopter kept moving. As soon as the light faded, he made a run for it. In a full sprint, he made his way to the deck and crawled through the opening of the lattice, and closed it behind him. As he made his move, soldiers were invading the back yard of the house. They looked around the yard but left when they saw that nobody was there.

"Nobody here, Bird's Eye." A soldier said into a walkie-talkie radio. They left out of the yard through a gate beside the house. We had to stay still because the ground was covered with loose gravel. I sat in wait and looked at my mom as she held a finger up to her lips. Poor Gordon had to sit in discomfort as the deck was not high enough from the ground for him to sit up straight. But he did not risk our safety so that he could get comfortable. Once the soldiers left the house, we waited a few minutes, silent and still as a stone, to assure they were really gone. Gordon and my mom nodded at one another, and he moved out from under the deck.

My mom made her way over to me and held me as tight as she could. She kissed me a few times on my head as she showed her joy that I was okay. Or she was just happy to still be alive. Suddenly, she heard movement. But in case it wasn't Gordon coming back to retrieve us, she became quiet again. The lattice moved, and Gordon poked his head in.

"Let's move!" he said. He held the lattice to the side as we exited the deck's underside and placed it back to decrease suspicion.

The Gem State Siege

In the dark, we ran around the side of the house and could see a line of soldiers sweeping the neighborhood. It seemed as if they were all marching to the entrance. This was our chance to head to the back of the community where our house was.

"We live back there."

"You want me to go first just in case there are still soldiers back there?" Gordon asked.

"No, we don't have time for that."

We hopped from yard to yard to keep from running out in the open. This was a good strategy because my mom was on the neighborhood watch. She knew exactly where all the hiding spots were. In case the helicopter came back, she knew exactly where to go in everyone's yard. When we reached the house two doors down from ours, my mom stopped running and stared off into the distance.

"Dr. Simms?" Gordon called out. "What's wrong?"

Without answering, my mom pointed across the street. One of the houses in our cul de sac was completely burned down. She hyperventilated as she stared at the burned-down residence. The smell of burned flesh filled the air, and my mom began to puke in the grass. Gordon reached out and pulled her hair back as a courtesy. The look on his face was a look of defeat as he stared at the house as well. Smoke still rising from the charred ruins of the like it had recently been extinguished. As much as my mother would have loved to stop running, she had to keep going, and that she did.

CHAPTER XII

We made our way inside the house. It was pitch-black dark inside, and almost impossible to grab our belongings.

"Shit!" My mom yelled as she stepped into the kitchen.

"What's wrong?" Officer Gordon asked.

"I'm fine. But those monsters actually cut the power to the grid."

"It's fine," he responded as he sorted through some stuff that my mother directed him to. "We won't be here long enough for luxuries."

"You're right, but this could cause other problems."

"Like what?"

"I'll let you know when they arise. I'll be back. Can you keep an eye on Milo for me?"

"Yeah, of course." He told her as she walked through the house.

Gordon scooped me up from the floor and sat me up on the kitchen counter. I watched him as he packed food items and essentials in a backpack.

"Do you know my daddy?" I asked him to break the silence.

"No, I'm afraid I don't. Why do you ask?"

"Because you like my mommy, don't you?" The rugged officer flinched. He coughed, then cleared his throat as he placed the backpack next to me. He put his hands on the counter and leaned against it. I could see him smile at me through the dim light of the candles and flashlights.

"That is a big accusation, Milo." He said to me. "I just met your mom, so I can't say that I like her in that way."

"But you think she's pretty?"

"Wait, hold up, little man!" He said as he zipped the bag. "Your mom is a married woman, and it is bad to look at a married person in that way."

"Good. Because I was going to tell my daddy to get you." I said to him, shaking a fist at him. Officer Gordon laughed at me and proceeded to pull me down from the counter.

"Gordon!" my mom yelled for him from down in the basement. It seemed urgent.

"Tawnie!?" He yelled back as he grabbed my hand and pulled me along. Once he got to the basement door, Gordon handed me a flashlight and told me to stay behind him.

"I'm fine! I just need your help with something!"

Gordon picked me up and walked down the steps. We found my mom moving furniture in the corner and uncovering a wall.

"All of this has to move." She said as she began to pull on one of the shelving units, dragging it across the concrete floor. The sound that it made was obnoxious and deafening. Worried that it could draw attention to us, Gordon stopped her from moving the shelf.

"Tawnie, wait!" He said to her, prying her hand off of the leg of the shelf. "We have to keep it down. Those men could be patrolling the neighborhood as we speak. If they happen to be walking around outside, we don't want them to hear us."

She looked at him with an inquisitive grin and nodded her head.

"Okay." She said as she walked back over to the wall. She stood there with a grin and sighed, staring at the furniture. "I need your help."

"What do you need?" The large man asked as he stepped behind her.

The Gem State Siege

"Not much of a luxury until you have to open it without power." She explained to him.

Gordon looked around, thinking that she would be referring to a safe. But she pointed to the wall.

"What the hell?" He asked. "There is a vault... here... in this wall?" My mother nodded and walked over to what appeared to be a control box.

"We have a bunker down here with supplies that we are definitely going to need."

"What supplies could we possibly need more than what we have?" Officer Gordon asked as my mom tore the cover from the control box. She grabbed a car battery from the corner and carried it over to the control box. She pulled a pair of what looked like jumper cables from it.

"What do you need me to do?" He asked her as he went to shine his light inside the control box.

"So, the lock is on a circuit that doesn't work without power. So I have to create a circuit that converts DC current to AC to trip the lock. Once that's done, I need you to push that handle as hard as you can so that the seal is broken. Once you push past the hydraulic system, it should slide open."

Officer Gordon got into position and waited for my mom to give him the signal.

"Ready." He said as she tinkered around with the battery and cables.

"You sure?" She asked him.

"Yup," He said as he braced himself. She began to count down from 5, and once she tripped the system, a spark came from the battery cables. Gordon pushed with all he had. My mom jumped up and saw that he almost had the seal broken and began to help him. As they got the door open, I saw the basement lights flicker for a moment before it turned on. I could see my mom's face as she stared at the bulb, utterly mortified.

"Oh shit!" Gordon said as he pushed the door open the rest of the way. Almost immediately, the light went back out.

"Gordon, hurry up and grab all you can!" My mom yelled at him.

"What am I grabbing?" He asked as he shined the flashlight into the vault. "Oh, sweet baby Jesus."

He was baffled as he saw what was inside the room. The vault was filled wall to wall, floor to ceiling, with nothing but artillery. He stood there with his mouth held open as he tried to get his words out.

"Gordon!?" My mom yelled for him to get him to move?

"Mommy, what's happening?" I asked.

"Milo, stay back and don't touch anything!" She yelled at me as she started to grab duffel bags and load them up with the guns.

"Why do you own this many guns?" Gordon asked her. For a moment, my mother gave him the angriest of looks.

"Did you not pay any attention to anything that happened today?"

Once my mom and Officer Gordon grabbed all they could take, we headed upstairs to leave out of the garage. Gordon looked out the windows on the garage doors and check for any visitors. My mom cocked a pistol and waited for him to give a signal.

"All clear." He said.

"Hurry, lift the garage door!"

The Gem State Siege

Officer Gordon removed the slide locks from the door, and my mom buckled me into the back of the hybrid car.

"Mommy, I'm scared," I said to her.

"We'll be fine, sweetie she said to me before closing the door. She hurried to toss the bags in the rear hatch and slammed it shut as she fumbled with keys to start the car. Of course, there was no sound to the engine. My mom was careful about driving out of the garage. Luckily, the car was facing forward. She was careful not to hit the brakes due to the light output in the pitch-black neighborhood. Upon exiting, she pulled the emergency brake to stay inconspicuous. Officer Gordon closed the garage door. He paused as he could see headlights coming up the hill of the neighborhood. In the sky, the helicopter was heading back towards the house.

"Gordon!" My mom screamed at him to get in. He snapped out of it and finally got in the car. My mom hit the gas and began to drive out of the cul de sac towards the oncoming vehicles. She was able to go down an alternate street without having to hit the brakes. We cleared the intersection in time to not be spotted by the helicopters above. A crowd of soldiers went to our house and went inside. We could see them from downhill as the helicopter shined its spotlight on the house. Fortunately for us, nobody followed.

My mom bolted through the residential neighborhood at about 40 miles an hour with a prayer in mind. She drove towards the neighborhood's back exit and could see lights shining. She headed down a dead-end street instead.

"Do you have a plan?" Officer Gordon asked as he held on to the handle above his head.

"I will when I get to it." My mom said to him.
"What does that even mean?"
"Just hang on!"

My mom found a dirt road at the end of the street and drove. Taking it slow and cautious, she used the light from the moon to see the road ahead. She knew that turning her lights on this close to the neighborhood would result in us being caught.
"You okay back there, Milo?" She asked me.
"Yes," I murmured, still afraid to speak.
"Do you know where this road goes?" Gordon asked.
"I'm pretty sure we can take it out to the main road." Mom answered. "I just want to get as far away from the situation as possible."
"Understood."

Gordon sat in silence for a moment and looked around for potential danger. Mom paid attention to the road ahead.
"Were you planning for this to happen?" He asked.
"What?"
"I was just wondering if you had plans to accommodate this happening."
"No, why do you ask.", My mom said as she looked over at him with much suspicion.
"You had enough ammunition to give to those guys and still have some left. The United States Armed Forces have fewer guns than you. What do you do for a living to help me understand the number of firearms you guys own.
"I guess, when you put it that way, I was prepared. I never wanted to be in trouble just in case something like this would take place."
"How could you possibly know that this would happen?"

The Gem State Siege

"I'm a psychologist, and I know people." She explained. "People always want me to evaluate a certain type of person. The person who is obviously mentally unstable. The person who has a long history of being mentally ill. It is easy to understand what that person is capable of. They are just that predictable. But the wealthy and the rich are never evaluated. It is almost as if no one truly believes that they can do bad things because they don't have to struggle for money. So when you actually pay attention, it's not hard to predict situations like this."

Officer Gordon's head fell, and he faced the front with my mom's words ringing in his ears.

She found the main road and stopped because she saw a vehicle coming in the distance.

"Shit!" My mom yelled as she looked back behind us. She turned towards the oncoming car and put the vehicle in park.

"What the hell are you doing?" Asked Gordon

"Hurry, put your seat down!"

The two of them did just that and hoped for the best as the vehicle drew closer. But upon closer inspection, it was definitely a soldier's vehicle."

The truck stopped in front of our car and began to shine lights on it. Tears began to fill my eyes as I unbuckled myself and slid down into the floor of the vehicle. My mom cocked the gun that she had and placed her finger in the trigger well.

"Have you ever shot a gun before?" Officer Gordon asked her.

"I don't have time to get a pep talk and shooting lessons." She said to him.

"If you do this, there is no turning back." A lone soldier

approached the car. Without warning, my mother jumped up and shot the man in the neck. The soldier fell to the ground clenching his wound. My mom immediately jumped out of the car and fired towards the vehicle. A man who stepped out of the truck was struck instantly. I screamed as I covered my ears to protect myself from the commotion. She walked over to the soldier and shot him in the forehead.

It was over. My mother stood on the side of the road, watching this man take his final breath. She then walked around to the back of our car and pulled the supplies out.
"What are you doing?" Gordon asked. But with no words, she came back and unbuckled me from my seat, and pulled me along to the black SUV. Gordon watched her as she led me over into the vehicle, and she got into the driver's seat without saying a word.

CHAPTER XIII

"You need to calm down." Officer Gordon said to my mother, unprovoked.

"What?"

"Your first is always the hardest."

It was now somewhere to the tune of 2am, and my mom looked back at me in the rear seat. And I must have been sleeping during this part.

"What do you mean?" She asked.

"I mean, it's hard to kill a man in cold blood and maintain a good, clean conscience." He explained.

"Am I really getting advice from the police on how to properly kill someone?"

"It takes an exceptional person to not feel anything after taking a life."

"I'm fine, Gordon." She said. "I did it to protect what is mine."

"And what exactly is yours?" He inquired.

"My life, my freedom, and my son. But you couldn't possibly know about that?"

"Did you assume that I don't have anything to fight for?"

"No, I assumed that a small town, racist Idaho Falls Police Officer was not big on values."

"You think you have all the answers, don't you?" He asked as he looked over at her with disgust in his expression. "How dare you be a psychologist and judge people the way you do?"

"I judge people because I'm a psychologist, not in spite of it."

"You know what? I will not argue with you." He said as

he turned away from my mother.

It had gotten quiet between the two of them for a while as they drove across the countryside. Neither of the two was willing to discuss why they were agitated. Yet, they couldn't avoid it either.

"What is your story, Officer Gordon?" My mom asked him. "I feel like if I knew you more, it would be easier to trust you."

"Trust? Is it really a good idea to trust anyone right now?"

"Look, I'm making an effort to extend an olive branch. You saved my life back in that school, so I do owe you."

"You don't owe me anything, Mrs. Simms." He said with a cold demeanor.

"Misses?!" My mom yelled in surprise. "We may have taken a step backward in our relationship."

"We do not have a relationship. We have a common purpose and a common goal. That is it."

"What is that?" She asked.

"To survive. We do not need to complicate this." Upset, my mother kept driving down the dark highway. For a while, she remained quiet as the two of them listened to one another breathing in the silent car ride.

"Are you always this tense." She asked him.

"Am I? I didn't notice."

"What is happening here? Wouldn't you rather be friends than enemies?"

"I would much rather not talk."

"Okay, I'm fully aware of the costs of being skeptical of people and why it is important. But if we are in this boat together, we may want to bond in the process."

"No need for bonding. I will be dropped off in Rexburg."

"Rexburg?" She said with much confusion. "Why Rexburg?"

"There is something that I need to take care of there."

"You have family there?" He remained silent. "Ahh. There is something I could use."

"You will drop me off and get as far away from there as possible."

"I'm sorry?" She said with a hint of attitude in her tone.

"I am better without you and your kid to look after while I fight these thugs."

"On your own? It would have saved you the time if you stayed at my house when they showed up."

Officer Gordon closed his eyes and took deep breaths as he tried not to say anything he would regret.

"Let's just take your family, and we will all get away from this madness." In response, he turned to my mother and stared at her with furrowed brows.

"I do not want you around me. I will stop in Rexburg and be out of your hair for good."

My mom smiled at him. The mysterious officer looked as if he was getting uncomfortable.

"The dark and broken personality. It's a wonder that you evaded me this long, Gordon. I used to piece together broken boys like you for fun."

"I am not your experiment. Do not start with me."

"I'm not here to be your enemy, Gordon." She said to him. "We have to tolerate one another at this moment, so we may as well make the best of it."

"Wouldn't it be best to just not talk?"

"No!" My mom said as she peeked in the mirror at me to see if I was still sleeping.

"There is no telling if we'll make it to see the sunrise. If I am to die, I will not do it with a stranger." She said.
"Why does that make a difference?" Gordon asked.
"I don't want to face death alone."

Officer Gordon looked over at my mom and saw how jumpy she was. Goosebumps covered her arms, and she shivered as she continued to check the rearview mirrors. She was afraid.
"Daniel." He said.
"What?" She asked as she looked back over at him. The two made eye contact as my mom inquired for him to clarify what he said.
"Daniel Gordon. I won't allow you to die alone." She smiled at him and turned back to the road ahead.

My mom chuckled as she reached up to wipe the tears from her eyes.
"What's so funny?" He asked.
"I get to die with the guy that pointed his gun at me yesterday. How ironic!"
He tensed up once more as he recalled that moment.
"Yeah, about that," he said. "I knew the attack was coming."
My mom got quiet and became serious as she looked over at him with her eyes wide.
"How?" She asked.
"We all knew that something wasn't right… but."
"But, what?" mom asked.
"Special forces guys were coming into town and policemen that we had never seen before."
He looked out into the distance with a blank stare.

"It was almost like..."

"They were preparing for something?" She asked him.

Gordon shook it off, grunting as he tried to cope with the possibility.

"Policemen were running a rescue operation that seemed to ask a lot of the wrong questions. Do you know an Officer Boulevardez?"

Gordon raised an eyebrow as he looked over at her again.

"I thought so."

"No, I do. But... he died almost seven years ago."

Mom noticed a change in his demeanor. He seemed like he was mumbling something under his breath. But his eyes seemed cagey as if he was in shock.

"You alright?" Then there was silence again.

"I'm no good at having people in my life. It will be best that we go our separate ways as soon as possible."

"Why do you feel that way?"

"Based on my own experiences, it may be best if we don't drag it out. I'll be cordial and hope that you successfully make it to your husband."

Hearing him say that, my mom raised an eyebrow at the man.

"Did I give you mixed signals or something?" She asked as she began to blush.

"No. It's not your fault." He assured her. Again, the two got quiet and continued to watch the road.

"How long have you two been together?" Gordon asked.

"It's been over ten years." She announced. "And Milo is five."

"I know," Gordon said as he chuckled.

"What?"

The Gem State Siege

"Milo told me that before telling me that I couldn't steal you away from his dad." She cringed from embarrassment. Gordon laughed.

"I am so sorry about that. I can not imagine how uncomfortable that was."

"No, it's okay." He assured her as he looked back at me. "He's a good kid."

"He definitely is." My mom responded as a tear fell from her eye.

"How are you feeling?" Gordon asked.

"Fine, why?" She responded. But instead of going back and forth with her, he just stared at her. After realizing what he was referring to, she got serious.

"Look, sometimes it's necessary to become the monster to defeat the monster."

"Unacceptable!" He yelled, shocking my mom into paying attention. She looked back at me to make sure that I was still asleep.

"You may be the one to psychoanalyze everyone, but I don't need a psych degree to see that you're better than that!" He explained.

My mother sat in silence and tried to keep driving. But she would have to pull off to the side of the road to get some fresh air.

"What are you doing?" Gordon asked as my mother bought the car to a halt and jumped out.

"Tawnie?" Gordon called out as he followed.

She started to pace the ground as she began to break down.

"Hey, what is it?" Gordon asked as he approached her. But she could not answer his question. Instead, she sobbed louder. Gordon, not knowing what to do, went to wrap his arms around her. She placed her head on his chest and started to unleash her pain. This catastrophe wasn't even the beginning. At this point, I had awakened and could see the stranger embracing my mother.

Unfortunately, their embrace was short-lived. In the distance, coming straight for us was another vehicle. Terrified, my mother stared as the headlights came closer.

CHAPTER XIV

My mom and Gordon ran back to the truck. While she ran back to the driver's seat, Gordon ran back to the rear hatch and opened it.

"Gordon, what the hell?" My mom screamed.

"Mommy, what's going on?" I asked.

"Everything is going to be fine, sweetie." She responded. Knowing it was a lie and she didn't really believe it either.

"Tawnie, I need you to get in the back and hide."

"What?" My mom yelled at him as he came back around the vehicle with a different shirt. In that short period, he had managed to find a uniform to dress like the soldiers.

"Tawnie, trust me." He said to her as the two of them stared at one another. The nonverbal understanding forced my mom to dive into the rear of the vehicle.

"Milo, get on the floor!" She yelled at me. I unbuckled myself and jumped onto the floor.

Officer Gordon jumped into the driver's seat and began to drive. I could see my mother's face underneath the seat. Just as Gordon approached the other vehicle, it flashed its high-beam lights. Gordon noticed the car slowing down. Reluctantly, he did the same. He saw the other vehicle had its window down. After we came to a complete stop, Gordon rolled his window down as well. My mom held a finger up to her lips, signaling me to stay quiet.

"What's up, battle? You good?" The man asked.

"Yeah, I'm good, battle. Just had to pull over and take a piss."

"I gotcha. There's not a bathroom or gas station for miles.

I've been marking my territory all up and down this road."

"Yeah, I feel ya."

"Where ya' headin'?" The soldier asked.

"Back to the base. Boss said he needs me up here for some special project."

"Lucky you!" The soldier said with excitement and a thick country accent. "I have to go down here with all the infected.

"Not really. All of the infected have been taken care of. What am I walking into up here?" Gordon asked.

"All of the potential reaches of this outbreak have been isolated, and we have control of the state now. But they think that other states were compromised."

Gordon took a hard swallow. Meanwhile, my mom was cocking her pistol in case there was a chance that she had to surprise the unsuspecting soldier.

"How many states are they suspecting? You know?" Gordon asked him.

"Nah, man. They say it's all the states touching Idaho."

"Just when we thought it was over."

"I know, right!"

"Alright, man, I gotta go. Can't keep the man waiting for me." Gordon joked.

"You are absolutely right about that." The two men laughed together and drove in opposite directions. When the coast was clear, my mom and I came back up.

"That could have gone a lot worse." Mom said as she hopped back into the passenger side of the vehicle.

"Yeah, we need to hurry up and get to the next town," Gordon responded.

"Why, what's wrong?"

"I have a bad feeling about this."

At that moment, mom turned around to look back at the soldier's vehicle in the distance. His brake lights still shined into the night as he sat for some reason on the deserted highway.

"He's not moving, Gordon!" She said with excitement.

"Shit!" Gordon responded.

My mom's started to panic. I could hardly see her expression through the darkness as she stared out the rear window.

"He's not moving yet!"

We were about two miles down the highway. Finally, the truck made a three-point turn and came back in our direction.

"No, no, no, no, no!" She yelled as she fumbled with her pistol.

"There's no way he could catch up to us, right?" She asked as she turned to look at Gordon.

"In normal circumstances, no." He responded.

"What do you mean by normal?" She looked ahead and became petrified. Another pair of headlights came towards us.

"Gordon?" My mom yelled at him.

"I have a plan," Gordon announced. "Hang on to something."

"Wait, what's happening?" She asked as Gordon took the vehicle into the left lane and floored the gas pedal.

"Gordon, what are you doing?"

"Just trust me!" He said as he braced himself to the steering wheel.

The Gem State Siege

Out of discomfort of the situation, my mom screamed and tucked herself into a ball. We soared down the road at 90 miles an hour in a crash course with another vehicle. I began to scream with my mom, not knowing what was happening.

"Gordon, stop!!!" But determined to carry out his plan, Gordon held his head low and peered out at the other vehicle as we drew closer. Inches before impact, Gordon swerved and swiped the other car. Which, I add, was yet another military SUV.

My mom spun around to assess the outcome of what Gordon just did. She could see the vehicle in the distance catching up to us somehow. The other vehicle that we hit had to do a three-point turn to come for us. This slowed the other car down and allowed us to gain some distance.

"We need a plan." Mom said.

"We get to Rexburg and lose them in the city," Gordon responded.

"No! We have to think ahead! If they are in the city, then there is no way they would let us in!"

"They're not!" Gordon said as he gave my mother a quick smile. "That guy was lying to us because he was on to us."

"How do you even know that?"

"I'm a police officer. I'm trained to tell if people are lying to me."

"You better hope you're right."

"If I'm not, then we won't have to worry about the infection at least. What's the plan?" He asked her. My mom pulled out another gun and rolled down the window.

"What the hell are you about to do?" Gordon asked.

"Let them catch up."

"What? You can't be serious!" he said as he began to

speed up.

"Gordon!" She called out once more. "If we take these guys into Rexburg with us, then it will cause us a lot of trouble that we don't need. We need to get rid of them before we get there."

Gordon thought on it for a while and slowed down a little to allow the other two vehicles to catch up. He knew that my mother was right. She always is. But her level of tenacity amid a dark situation was impressive to him.

"You're not going to..." He began to ask as he saw her stand up through the window and sit on the door frame.

"Keep it steady!" She yelled to him as she knocked on the roof of the vehicle.

"This is not happening right now," Gordon grumbled as he continued to speed down the road.

The first shot let off from the nine-millimeter pistol chamber. The car behind us swerved as the bullet hit their windshield.

"Hold the damn car straight, Gordon!" She yelled.

"I'm trying!" He yelled back to her as he looked into his rearview mirror to gauge how far they were. She let off another single shot.

"Pow!" The gun sounded off. She put her training to use and practiced a technique that she had been working on for a while.

"Pow, pow, pow, pow, pow, click." The gun sounded off as she emptied the clip.

"Shit! Milo, get me another clip!" She yelled into the car.

"He's five!" Gordon yelled. I started to undo my seat belt, and I bravely jumped back into the back of the SUV.

"Grey bag, left, side pocket!" She yelled.

"Got it!" I said as I climbed back over to the front seat

with three clips of bullets in hand.

"I'll be damned," Gordon said as he looked and watched me hand the clip to my mom. Suddenly, the car hit a bump, and she dropped the clip.

"Got dammit, Gordon!" She yelled.

"That was a coyote!"

"Mommy, here!" I yelled out to her as I handed over another clip. She reached in and took it from my hand and put it in the pistol with expert level precision.

Once she was locked and loaded, she began to shoot at the car's window again. Eventually, the window shattered, and my mom got a clear shot at the driver. She was down to the last shot, and she awaited the perfect opportunity to let the final round out of the clip.

"Nice and steady, Gordon!" She yelled into the car.

"Straight stretch!" He responded.

"Pow!" The pistol went off. Suddenly, we could hear the engine rev in the car behind us as he rolled off to the side of the highway.

"Boom!" My mom said with excitement after realizing that she hit her mark.

"Do not get cocky! We still have one left."

My mom got back in the car and said for me to put my seatbelt back on.

"I see a sign coming up," Gordon said. "Rexburg, 3 miles."

"We have to shake this guy before we get there." She said as she looked back behind us. "Shit, he's catching up!"

"How?"

The second vehicle had somehow caught up, despite

The Gem State Siege

Gordon having the gas pedal smashed to the floor.

"Did you run out of bullets?" Gordon asked.

"Unfortunately. What are we going to do?" My mom responded. Suddenly, the vehicle slammed into the back of us and tried to perform a pit maneuver. Luckily, Gordon had experience with this himself, a cop who has had a few high-speed chases in his day. The back end of our vehicle swung to the right, but Gordon managed to bring it back to the center. Quickly, my mom jumped back into the back seat and reached over into the cargo area.

"I may have something that could help." My mom said as she rummaged through the bags in the back. Suddenly, we were slammed from behind again.

"Aaah!" My mom screamed.

"You guys, okay?" Gordon asked as he kept his eyes on the road. My mom leaned over to check on me before answering, "For now."

The damage to the back of our vehicle was surprisingly great. The rear hatch began to pop open, and my mom found herself looking into the headlights.

"Uh, Gordon?" She called out as she quickly pulled out a gun and pointed it at the other vehicle.

"Hang on!" Gordon yelled back as the other truck rammed us again. This time, Gordon lost control of the car, and we spun around on the road. As our vehicle slid off to the highway, we flipped as soon as our tires met the dry desert dirt.

Despite flipping twice and still landing right-side-up, we were all still alive. My mom, being the only one of us unbuckled, was injured pretty bad. Gordon had hit his head on something upfront, and he was disoriented but still awake. Whether he was alert or not was negotiable.

"Mommy, mommy!" I called out. But she could not answer right away as the pain hit her.

"Milo, you okay?" She asked me.

"Yes." I quickly responded. The headlights of the other vehicle slowly filled our cabin as he pulled up in front of us. From where I sat, I could see the man get out of the SUV and look in our direction. It almost seemed as if he looked me directly in the eyes. I remember thinking that this was the moment we die. Can you imagine how that thought reciprocates through the mind of a 5-year-old?

The man reached back into his truck, pulled out a big rifle, and immediately pointed at our vehicle.

"If you are still alive, no need to make this hard." The guy stated as he slowly approached. "I just want to know how you got my partner's truck." At this point, I unbuckled myself and got down onto the floor with my mother. We waited for the inevitable to happen. The soldier saw that Gordon was disoriented and walked around to the driver's side of the vehicle. Gordon tried to hold the door closed, but the man was stronger at this moment. He ripped the door open and hit him in the jaw with the buttstock of the gun. Blood splattered from Gordon's mouth and all over the vehicle dashboard.

The soldier yanked him out of the car and pointed his weapon at him.

"Not so funny now, huh, punk?" The man said to him as he attempted to crawl away, watching him struggle to his feet. Gordon made it up to a vertical base and faced the soldier. The brave police officer closed his eyes and waited for his end. As he knew, fighting the armed gunman would be futile in his current condition.

The Gem State Siege

As the soldier was preparing to pull the trigger and put Gordon out of his misery, "POW!" A single gunshot was heard.

Gordon realized that the caliber of the gunshot couldn't have come from that rifle. With the will of a stubborn mule, she managed to shoot the attacker from behind. Once Gordon realized what had happened. He limped over to catch my mom as she began to fall to the ground.

"Tawnie!" He called out to her as he pulled her close. "Tawnie, are you okay?" My mom closed her eyes and smiled as she said, "We're even now, Daniel."

CHAPTER XV

Gordon loaded me into the other car. He tried his best to shield my eyes from the dead body. The scene was well lit by the headlights of both vehicles. He made me put my seat belt on, and he closed the door to the SUV. Gordon then limped over to my mother and helped her up from the ground. He put my mom in the front seat of the car and leaned her back. She moaned and groaned in pain. He then closed the door and headed back to the other vehicle.

"Mommy?" I called out to her. "Are you okay?"

"I'm fine, love. I just need some rest now." She responded, trying to hide her pain.

Gordon returned to the car with the bags we brought from the house and put them in the rear. He then slammed the door shut and walked to the front of the truck. I could see him as he squatted in front of the vehicle, but I was too short to see what he was doing.

A few minutes later, Gordon jumped back in and hurried to pull away from the scene. As we backed away from the other vehicle, I could see it burst into flames.

"What's the rush?" My mom asked him.

"You have internal bleeding that needs attention," Gordon told her. As young as I was at the time, I remembered assuming that my mom was about to die.

"Mommy!" I cried out.

"Milo, I'm fine! Quiet down!" She said to me. "How could you possibly know that?"

"I used to be a medic."

"You have got to be shitting me!"

"I am a man of many experiences." He joked.

The Gem State Siege

"Well, I don't think you should be driving with a concussion."

We headed for the town, and luckily, the rest of the night went well.

It was the following morning where things got interesting. We spent most of it in Madison Memorial Hospital as my mom and Officer Gordon had their wounds tended to. I sat in the waiting room of the hospital's emergency room with him, and he seemed to be on edge the entire time. My mother was being seen in the triage for a fractured rib.

The day seemed bright and sunny. All seemed well in the city. It seemed strange that no military presence showed up. Showing on a nearby television was a news broadcast reporting the burned vehicle on the outskirts of town. I looked up at Gordon, and he looked down at me.

"You good kid?" He asked me, seeming exhausted.

"Yes, sir," I responded. "I just want my mommy."

"Yeah, I know. But she will return. Your mom is tough."

He placed his hand on the top of my head to comfort me. "I think that's why you are so tough."

I was starting to take a liking to Gordon. Even though I hardly knew him. I felt like he was more comfortable to be around than my own dad. Suddenly, a doctor came out and called for Gordon. He grabbed me, and we both walked over to him as he stared down at a clipboard.

"Mr. Gordon, your wife has been subjected to—"

"Wait, Doc, she's not my wife." Gordon frantically said.

"Oh, I just assumed... I'm so sorry!" The doctor responded.

"No, it's fine. This is her son." He said as he introduced

me to the doctor. "Let's not talk in front of the kid, Doc."

"Oh, yes, of course."

Just as they were walking away, I called out to the doctor.

"Doctor, is my mommy going to die?" I asked him with tears in my eyes. The doctor lent me a slight smile as he approached me. He kneeled in front of me, placed his hand on my shoulder, and looked me square in the eyes. With a smile on his face, he assured me that she was fine and in good hands. She was, but there was something, of course, that he did not disclose to the five-year-old that he had to tell someone. The next possible candidate to receive the information was Officer Gordon. The doctor stood back up and walked over to the entrance of the emergency room to speak privately. I jumped back up into a chair and watched the two men as they spoke, hoping to get more info on my mom from either of them. I noticed the doctor showing Gordon papers with charts on them. The silky sheen of the X-ray gleamed underneath the fluorescent lighting. Periodically, Gordon looked back to check on me. An indication that the conversation wasn't good. The doctor finished, and Gordon, with his hands in his pockets, watched him walk away. He almost seemed remorseful and reluctant to turn around. But eventually, he did. He came over to me and began to pick up the coloring book and bag of chips I received from the nurse.

"Alright, kid, let's go see your mommy!"

Entering the triage, I looked around for my mom but got worried as I saw everyone but her. Officer Gordon calmly walked the halls. His eyes carefully scanning each room number as he walked past. He took me towards the back and found the room numbered 2G. He pushed the wide door open and stood aside to allow me in. As soon as I passed him, I could see my mother inside putting her shoes on.

"Mommy!" I yelled as I ran to her.

"Hi, sweetie!" She smiled at me. I chose not to hug her in fear of hurting her. So I stood in front of her and began to tear up.

"Aww, Milo." She said as she pulled me in to hug me.

"It'll be okay. I'm not going anywhere." As she held on to me, she looked up at Gordon and smiled as her lips formed to say "thank you." But despite her smile, she could see the pain in his eyes as he watched her. It was then that she knew that there was a conversation that needed to be had. So have that conversation they did. But we'll get to that later.

Once my mother gathered all their belongings and checked out of the hospital with me at her side. We stepped out the door to see Gordon already waiting at the truck. We approached the vehicle. Gordon opened the passenger door for my mom, and then he walked around the SUV and opened my door. I climbed in and buckled myself up as usual. When I looked up, my mom was staring at me with a smile on her face. It was a smile of content. A look that I hadn't seen in a while. There may have been something on her mind at the moment. But it may have been the drugs from the hospital to ease the pain of the two broken ribs that she had. Unflinching and not blinking, she stared, and I grew uncomfortable. But something was happening that I could not explain. Until it was too late.

Gordon jumped back in the car and started it up. He looked around at the two of us and proceeded to drive away from the hospital.

"Where are we going, Gordon." She asked him.

"I have some friends here in the city. We'll go to them and rest up until we come up with a plan."

My mom looked at him with longing eyes. However, he did not look at her at all. He simply watched the road and did not acknowledge her.

"Is everything okay?" She asked him.

"Everything is good. Why wouldn't it be?" He responded.

"It's just... You're just..." My mom started to say. I could tell, even then, that she was getting emotional. "I just want to say thank you."

"For what?"

"For saving me... And taking this journey with me."

"Don't mention it. I would much rather see you and your son live at the end of this." He responded, still not looking over to her. My mother began to fidget with her hands as she grew uncomfortable at the moment.

"So what happened to your husband?" Gordon asked. My mom, not expecting the question, looked at him with a befuddled look on her face. Gordon then looked down at her left hand, where she sported a shiny wedding band with diamonds in it. My mom looked down at the ring and then back to me. She noticed that I was paying close attention to their conversation.

"Milo's dad is a complicated man." She said to him. "Despite how much of an asshole he is, I wish I knew where he was. Or even if he's safe."

"You haven't talked to him since all of this started?"

"No."

"Why? If I were in a relationship, I would need to know everything, down to longitude and latitude."

"Yeah, me too," Mom mumbled.

"What does that mean? Why can't you call him?"

"I can't call him because it keeps going to voice mail." I could see the tears running down her face, and Gordon noticed it as well.

"Where was he?"

She took a second to wipe away her tears before answering.

"He was working on a research assignment in Yellowstone."

"So he's probably safer than us right now, to be honest." Gordon joked. "So I wouldn't be too worried."

"You're probably right."

"Where did you meet?" He asked. Making my mom give him a look of confusion.

"Do you really want to know, or are you just trying to small talk me?" She asked.

"I don't do small talk. I just want you to talk about it."

My mom sat, quiet for a moment, as she stared out the window at the scenery. She thought back on their relationship.

"We met in high school, 2006," Mom announced.

"2006?" Gordon asked in surprise. My mom leaned with an eyebrow raised as she stared at him in suspicion. "What year did you graduate?"

"2006."

"Oh, wow."

"Excuse you?" She said with a grin on her face.

"I just didn't think you were that old."

"Ah!" She gasped. "How rude!"

"No! You look good for your age. I just wouldn't have guessed you'd be older than me."

"What the hell?"

"No, I'm saying that I thought you were much younger." He groveled his case.

"Okay, thanks, I guess." She said as she crossed her arms

and gave him an attitude.

"How long did it take for you to say it first?"

"Say what first?"

"The L Word?"

"How'd you figure I said it first?" She asked as she laughed.

"I think I can tell that much about you now." My mom was now in tears as she laughed about her and my dad's history with a mixture of Gordon's antics.

"How long were you in the Army?" She asked him.

"Ten years ago, I left my home to join the Army. I spent eight years in, then I was discharged and headed to the police force." He answered.

"So you are just as old but felt the need to make me feel like an antique?" She asked as the two of them laughed together for a moment.

The conversation eventually died down, and my mom went back to looking out of the window.

"Whatever bought you guys together, remember those things," Gordon said to her. She turned to him with eyes full of tears. "Big or small, everything good should be cherished long before you count your bad,"

I trusted Gordon because he showed that he was not interested in my mom romantically. I didn't really understand their bond until later in life, however.

"Enough about me." Mom said as she wiped her eyes again. "What about the silent police officer with the bad attitude. What good do you cherish?"

"None." He said. My mom was startled at his direct answer. "I tried that once. It didn't work."

"Awww." She squealed with her hands clasped together at her mouth. "You were actually in love once."

The Gem State Siege

I looked at him in the rearview mirror as he laughed with my mom for a moment. Suddenly, his entire expression changed as he began to reach deep for a pain that he had locked away.

"What happened?" My mom finally asked.

"She was killed." He said to her as he began to grind his jaw. Suddenly, I began to feel something again. Just like before on the highway in Idaho Falls. I began to feel this rising sensation all over my body as if I was falling. It felt like heat and cold at the same time, and it could not be ignored. It gradually came to me, and it faded away slowly. Afraid of what could happen next, I said nothing to warn my mom of what I felt.

"What happened to her? If you don't mind me asking."

"There was a car accident. The car rolled off the cliffside, and she was ejected during the roll. The car landed on top of her and killed her on the spot." He explained.

"Oh, no! I'm so sorry!" Mom said with her hands covering her mouth. "How long ago?"

"Ten years."

My mom took a hard swallow as she put the math together and realized precisely why Gordon was like this.

"What was her name?" She asked him.

"Terrie." He answered with a look of despair on his face.

"You think that Terrie would want you to keep hanging yourself up about her death?"

Gordon shrugged his shoulders and just kept driving. My mom sat in her seat, silent, staring at him. She tried reaching for his hand, and he immediately pulled away.

"She probably would." He finally answered.

"Why would you say that?" My mom asked. "That is

exactly why—"

"Because I was driving the car." He interrupted her. My mom looked at him with her mouth and eyes wide open as she struggled to find what to say next. "There was ice on the roads, and she never wanted to leave in fear of something like that happening."

My mom sat back and paid attention as he finally opened up to her.

"I remember telling her once that I would take her to see the world and show her new experiences in life. I showed her a new experience and the last one. I even called her paranoid and crazy just before I dragged her out of the house that night."

"Wait, you shouldn't…" Mom started to argue with him. "Okay. I understand." She said as she gave in to what he was saying.

"No psychanalysis this time?" He asked.

"No. I completely understand." Mom told him. "No matter how much I tell you otherwise, you will never reach acceptance until you want to reach it."

"Mommy, I'm hungry," I interjected to stop the conversation. My mom looked back at me and smiled. I playfully raised my hand to her, and she began to giggle.

"Hey, I won't get on you because you are grown, and I feel like you know better. But there is one thing about acceptance and forgiveness that you need to know." Mom explained to him. "You have to forgive yourself to receive forgiveness."

"What if I can't do it?" He asked. "What if I was meant to be in misery because of this?"

"Nobody deserves to be in pain the way you are."

CHAPTER XVI

Before noon, we were pulling up at a house on the west side of the city.

"Who's house is this?" My mom asked.

"That friend that I was telling you about," Gordon answered as he stepped out of the truck.

"Is this someone that you served with?"

"Yeah, met way back in basic," Gordon answered as he opened the rear door and helped me out. We all approached the house together. As soon as we stepped on the porch, Gordon rang the doorbell. As we waited, my mom looked around the neighborhood.

"Something wrong?" Gordon asked her.

"Not really?" Mom said as if she wasn't even sure herself. "It feels like I've been to this neighborhood before, but I can't honestly remember."

The door opened, and a large black man stood there with a wide Cheshire Cat-style grin on his face. Immediately, Gordon lit up like a child that found his best friend. My mom looked at him, dumbfounded at the energy that he was now giving off. The man unlocked the glass outer door and opened it.

"Gordon!" The huge man growled.

"Francie!" Gordon responded as he stepped into the house first and embraced the man with immense joy.

"Come in, come in!" The man yelled as he still hugged Gordon. The two men were too joyous to let go of one another. My mother and I stepped inside the house and immediately began to smell food. Both of us took a big whiff of the air inside the home. We looked at one another with excitement. My mom held her finger up to me as we shuffled to the side to get out of the way. I could see a woman walking into the foyer. Small but elegant, she gracefully stepped into the front of the house with a smile on her face.

"And that must be none other than the infamous Gordon!" She yelled.

"Vick!" Gordon yelled as he let go of the man and went to pick up the little gorgeous, blonde woman. My mom bashfully stood there, waiting for the group to settle down and acknowledge her. Eventually, the extended greetings ended, and finally, the little woman looked at my mom and me.

"Ah." The woman said in astonishment as she smiled at my mom and approached us. "Hi!"

"Hi." My mom said as she reached out to shake the woman's hand.

"I am so sorry for being rude!"

"No, it's fine!"

"Victoria." The woman introduced herself.

"I'm Tawnie, and this is my son M.J." The men came back over.

"This is my husband—"

"Lester France!" The man excitedly interrupted his wife as he reached for my mom's hand.

"Come in, make yourselves comfortable, folks," Victoria said as she strutted into the kitchen. "Are you guys hungry?"

Immediately, I followed the woman into the kitchen.

"Milo?" My mom called out to me.

"Excuse me!" I yelled up to the woman in the kitchen. "Huh?"

"I was wondering if I can have some breakfast?"

"Oh my god!" She squealed as she picked me up from the floor and walked to the front of the house. "You have raised him so well!"

"I'm so sorry!" My mom said as she blushed.

"No worries! No need to apologize." She said as she placed me back on the floor. "His manners are refreshing." She said as she side-eyed her husband. She then got down to a knee and addressed me. "Of course, you can have some breakfast, my good fellow. As long as you go with your mommy and get freshened up."

Victoria looked up at my mom and nodded.

"Thank you so much!" My mom said as I walked over. Victoria showed us to the restroom in the master suite, and Gordon went to the other. My mom was almost the same size as the tiny woman, so she left out a shirt and a pair of black leggings for her to put on. My mom knew to grab me a change of clothes when we were at our home the night before. When we finished, we walked back out into the dining area, and my mom sat me down at the table.

"Can I help with something?" She asked the couple.

"Absolutely not!" The man said as he urged my mom to sit down. "You need help with anything, love?" He asked Victoria as he walked into the kitchen.

At this point, Gordon was joining us from the back. There was a television nearby that showed the news. It was a broadcast of yesterday's events.

"So, I heard about what happened," Victoria said as she bought us plates with a generous amount of food. My eyes grew large, and my smile grew more prominent as I stared at the plate in joy. A hefty amount of fried potatoes sat next to scrambled eggs, bacon, and pancakes. I was in heaven. Eventually, the couple had their plates in hand and came to join us at the table.

"Yeah, I'm still trying to wrap my head around it all." My

mom responded.

"I think it is interesting what the news is saying right now," Lester said.

"Yeah... Apparently..." My mom was starting to say as she looked down at me. She was reluctant to have any of this conversation in front of me.

"Hey, Milo!" Victoria called me, taking my attention away from the food in front of me. "Do you want to watch some cartoons while you eat?"

"Yes, please!" I said as I tapped my mom's leg and got down from the chair. The woman reached over to my mom for the plate and walked me over into the living room where the television was. She grabbed the remote and immediately changed the channel.

"What did the news say?" My mom asked.

"Apparently, there is a disease the government is looking to contain before it spreads," Victoria answered.

"But, the funny thing is, they can't say what the disease actually is or where it came from," Lester added.

"They came into Idaho Falls and shut the entire city down," Gordon added. "Everyone there is..."

"No way!" Victoria cried out. "Why did the police let that happen?"

"They didn't. This militant group rolled into town and completely decimated the police department. Everyone who wore the badge is dead."

"I'm glad you made it out, man," Lester said to him.
"Me too."
"How did you get out?" Victoria asked.
"I was at the shelter tending to those who were affected by the earthquake."
"Earthquake?" Lester questioned.

"What earthquake?" Asked Victoria. "The news didn't say anything about an earthquake."

"The entire ground shook apart, and fire shot up from the ground like the geysers in Yellowstone. I think the entire Western side of Idaho Falls is completely destroyed."

Victoria looked at her husband with an eyebrow raised.

"What's wrong?"

"We have a friend who told us about some conspiracy yesterday. He said something similar," Lester answered. "We ignored it and called him crazy."

"We never wanted to believe that the government would respond to a disease with extermination." Said Victoria.

They sat at the table without saying a word as their thoughts ran wild. But Gordon frowned as a thought hit him.

"Tawnie, did you see anyone with a mask or face covering on?" He asked.

"No... I didn't." She answered. But now, she was in the same frame of mind.

"What kind of disease is this contagious that an entire city needs to be murdered but isn't airborne?"

"Could it be something in the water?" Lester asked.

"No telling," Gordon answered.

"Hey, Lester." My mom called out. "When you and Gordon served, did you two ever hear about the military doing anything like this before now?"

"Oh!" Lester smiled. My mom looked confused as Lester and Gordon both dropped their heads.

"It was actually me who served with Gordon," Victoria said.

"How did I get that wrong?" My mom asked as she looked around at the table, embarrassed.

"It was probably their sickening bromance."

"Hey, all jokes aside..." Gordon said to bring the conversation back around. "In no time of the constitution has this ever been allowed to happen. But these people are not military. At least not the United States Military. They're all too sharp. When I was in the school dealing with them, it felt like I was in the special forces program again."

"That bad?" Victoria asked. He nodded his head and took a deep breath. "Do you think this is what they were talking about?" Victoria paused.

My mom looked at both of them with concern.

"What are you guys talking about?" She asked.

"There was a mission that we deployed at the end of my career, where we were tasked to do something horrible. I think this is that mission coming back to bite us in the ass." Gordon explained. Suddenly, the doorbell rang, and I saw a face that I was excited to see and ran to the glass door.

"Daddy!" I yelled as everyone got up from the table and came into the foyer. He entered the house and wrapped his arms around me tightly.

"My son." He whispered as tears filled his eyes.

"Milo?" My mom called out to my disheveled father. He ran over to her and kissed her passionately. The two were reunited once more. But what bought them together again was just as important as what tore them apart.

CHAPTER XVII

My mother pushed my father off of her and stepped back.

"As awkward as this situation is, I'm glad you're here, Milo.", Victoria said to my father as he stared at my mother in shock. "Come get cleaned up."

"Wait, you two know one another?" My mom asked her.

"Milo is the crazy friend we told you about earlier," Lester explained. "We crossed paths a few years ago when I was assigned to escort him and his team on a secret mission."

"Escort?"

"Yes, I'm a cop."

"Yup, that explains a lot."

"Tawnie, I thought you were dead." My dad said.

"What? Why?"

"I saw what happened to Idaho Falls. I thought you were in the middle of it."

"The disaster that you guys told us about?" Victoria asked. "Do you know what happened?"

A car started to come down the street. He got paranoid and hid behind the door frame, all while peeking outside.

"Milo, what is your problem?" Victoria asked.

"Those men, the ones in black, they're coming for me." He said.

"Wait, they are after you too? Who are they?" Gordon asked him.

"I can explain." My dad said as he slammed the door shut. "We have to lock down the house. One of their cars is already here!"

"You missed that on the way in?" Lester asked. "That's theirs."

"Enough!" My mom yelled. "What are you freaking out about?"

"The end is here, and those men are the ones that will bring it!"

"Well, are you going to explain to us what's going on?" Lester asked.

My dad began to frantically look around his feet for his bag. He grabbed it up from the floor and quickly unzipped it. I could see my mom unimpressed as she stared at him. He pulled out a laptop and ran into the living room, and plugged in the charger cable. We followed and crowded around him. My dad started the computer up and pulled up an aerial image of Idaho Falls.

"Now I wasn't ready to see this, and I wasn't even there. Are you sure you want to see it?" He asked my mom.

"Yes." She answered him with a slight attitude.

He showed the video, and all of us were baffled. None of us had any idea of how bad the situation had gotten until we saw that video.

"That is insane!" Lester said as he wiped the sweat from his forehead and sat down on the couch.

"That is what they're hiding?" Gordon asked.

"I think I'm going to be sick," Victoria said as she walked into the kitchen.

My mother walked away, lost in thought. The screen paused on the symbol created by the fire. The other three adults in the room talked among one another as she stared at the screen.

"Tawnie, have you seen this before?" My dad asked. Everyone looked at her, who seemed disconnected for a moment.

"I have." She stepped forward.

"What does it mean?" Victoria asked.
"It means that we have reached our final days."
"What?" Gordon and my dad yelled.
"Victoria, what mission were you guys talking about earlier?" She asked.

My mom stepped forward, closed the laptop without words, and turned around to look at them. She seemed serious. As if she knew something or had something heavy on her mind.
"You guys were a part of that mission?" She asked them.
"What mission?" My dad asked.
"You guys were the ones that found the temple weren't you?"
Gordon looked at her in shock. My mother looked up to the ceiling while biting her lower lip in frustration.
"I'm sitting here listening to you guys and realized how all of you... All of us know one another."
"What are you talking about?" Victoria asked.
"None of this is just a coincidence."
"What?" Asked Lester.
"We are all written in history as people involved with that symbol and the chaos that is to come of it." She said.
"I'm confused, love." My dad said to her.
"Let's go back to the beginning." She started to explain as she sat down on the couch. "Four years ago, a young psychologist blows the cover off of a secret operation. An operation that was so top secret that people involved were killed to tie loose ends. A group of ten soldiers and a few archaeologists are responsible for going into a forbidden temple. Their mission, to find a jewel that was not supposed to be found."

As the story started to unfold, everyone grew more uncomfortable.

"You two were on that team."

Gordon and Victoria both dropped their heads.

"Somehow, the energy inside the temple turned the scientists into deranged psychopaths. They killed seven of the ten soldiers. But later killed by the three survivors. An unlucky scientist and his police escort take the package to Primotech. They hand over the most dangerous weapon in the world to a corrupt agency that had no good intentions for it! Or the rest of mankind, for that matter!"

"What does this mean?" Victoria asked.

My mom went to her bag and pulled out a notebook, and flipped through the pages until she reached a sketch of the symbol. My dad began to sweat as he locked his eyes on the drawing.

"That doesn't necessarily mean that they are after us," Gordon said. "What about the quarantine?"

"I think I can answer that. I think I know who those men are." My dad said.

"We established that, right?" Lester asked. "They're Primotech"

"Nope." Mom said to him, shaking her head.

"Primotech wants to weaponize people with powers," Dad announced. "They used the thing that came from the temple to create humans with extraordinary abilities."

"Extraordinary abilities?" Lester interrupted. "That is insane!"

"I want to agree with you, Lester. But, this is something that I have seen with my own eyes." My dad opened the laptop again and began to play a video of a soldier that appeared to be on fire.

"It's real, France." My dad said to him.

"Big deal, a guy on fire. It's still not—" He paused. The man on the video began to throw the flames from around his body into whichever direction he wanted.

"How did you get that?" Mom asked my dad.

"I uploaded it onto a flash drive while nobody was looking." My dad told her. "Primotech wants to create super soldiers with this energy. However, the radiation leaked into the surrounding areas."

"Including Idaho Falls," Mom added.

"How did you come to the conclusion that this group, Primotech, is after us?" Gordon asked.

"I figured all of this out in a matter of minutes." She explained as she began to pace. "Your names rang in my ears as if I already knew who you were, and it turns out, I did."

"That didn't answer my question."

"You're right. I imagined that the other survivor of the temple is in trouble too. What do you think?" she asked as she took my dad's laptop to use.

"Yeah, exactly." Victoria cheerfully said." In that case, we will all be fine."

My mom turned the laptop around and showed an obituary post about Sergeant Tyson Conner.

"Tyson Conner was killed two weeks before all of this by some unknown circumstances. And to answer your question, we are now the last ones with knowledge of this." My mom explained.

Victoria gasped and covered her mouth with her hands. Gordon suddenly appeared frantic at the news as he held his jaw in disbelief.

"What are we going to do?" Victoria asked as she began to clutch her head in her palms. "We can't possibly stop an entire army."

My dad then got up to grab his bag again, and he looked at it in wonder.

"Milo?" Victoria called out? "What's wrong with you?"

My dad reached down into his dusty, tattered backpack and slowly pulled out something. My mother waited in anticipation as he fumbled around in the bag for a moment. We began to see a bright, orange glow inside the bag. He had pulled out a red orb that lit the room.

"What is that?" I asked, mesmerized by the light it gave off.

"It's the freaking Pyro Stone." My angry mother answered.

CHAPTER XVIII

"What the hell, Milo?!" My mom screamed. "Why the hell do you have that?"

"I didn't want it to be used as a weapon anymore!" He screamed back as he paced about the room, staring at the relic.

"There are probably kaitron monitors all around us right now. You've brought the source of infinite power right into the den of loose ends."

"I didn't know!" My dad stammered.

"Kaitrons?" Lester and Victoria asked.

"The measurement of energy emitted from living organisms." She answered as she began to look out the blinds. "We have to move."

"What, why?" Victoria asked.

"Because if we stay, they will find that and ultimately find us!" My mom answered.

"Wait, Tawnie, are you suggesting we leave that here?" Gordon asked her.

"We can't have that with us. We'll be a moving beacon if we do."

"Maybe, but would you be okay giving it to the enemy?" My dad asked. "We can fight to keep them from getting it."

"Your entire brand is built on showing the world the truth about the corruption in our country. If you weren't going to do it to save your fellow man, why even do it?" Gordon asked.

My mom's head fell as she tried to think of a response. She walked into the kitchen as she fell deep into her thoughts.

"Hey. What's going on?" Gordon asked as she pretended to ignore him.

"Tawnie, look at me." He persisted. My mom turned to look at him. Everyone else in the room stared at the two.

"You know what we need to do." He said to her.

"We couldn't possibly stand up to this organization, Danny." She said as she walked away from him. But he followed her.

"Listen, if we don't fight to at least warn the world about this organization, we can't say what may happen for sure."

"Tawnie!" My dad called out as he walked into the kitchen. "You've worked hard...too hard to give up now."

My mom looked at him with worry as she stared at the relic. Finally, she took a deep breath and leaned against the counter. The other adults walked into the kitchen to join the conversation.

"Milo, what exactly do we know about that thing?" Mom asked.

"What do we do with it?" Lester asked.

"Give it to the authorities?" Victoria asked apprehensively.

"Honestly, at this point, we are the authorities," Mom added.

"She's right," Gordon interjected. "We are up against a group that has their hands in the government's pocket. We can't trust anyone."

"So, what's the plan?" Dad asked.

"Do we keep running? Or do we figure out a way to get this burden off our backs?"

"It doesn't matter." My mom said as she left the kitchen to grab her belongings.

"What are you doing?" My dad asked her as he walked

The Gem State Siege

into the living room behind her.

"I am getting my stuff, including my son, and I am leaving here before those thugs get here."

"How do you know that they are coming for us, exactly?" Lester asked.

My mother looked at the others and shook her head.

"How would you like me to convince you, Lester?" She asked. "Do you want me to call them and ask if they are really looking for this shiny red thing that my husband stole? Or we can keep it and hide it in the Christmas tree lights."

"Tawnie, what's gotten into you?" My dad yelled at her.

"Oh, you want to know what's gotten into me? Huh?!" She said as she dropped her bag on the hardwood floor and stepped to my dad. "I am sick of you, causing all type of chaos in my life!"

Everyone stopped as she screamed at him. I began to cry as I saw my parents going at it like the bitterest of rivals. This was not the first time I heard them arguing. But this time felt different, not because of the tension between them. Now, they didn't sound like a married couple anymore. They seemed to be more like enemies this time around. The others tried to intervene and bring them both to their respective corners.

"You guys need to calm down!" Victoria said as she pulled Tawnie back. Suddenly, something happened that made my mother completely freeze. After the men pulled my father away, she stood still in shock for a moment. Gordon saw the look on her face and felt obligated to check on her.

"Tawnie, what's wrong?" He asked her.

As everyone got quiet, she looked around the room. I remember getting scared as I started to get that feeling again.

"They're here." My mom said as she walked towards the

window, careful not to make any noise.

"What?" Victoria asked. "Who's here?"

Outside, we began to see shadows walking past the windows in front of the house. My mother held up a finger as Lester lifted the kitchen island's countertop and pulled out weapons.

"Milo, hide." She whispered to me. I got down from the couch and scurried over to hide in a hallway closet. Lester handed guns out to everyone in the room. All I could hear from inside the closet was the clicking of their weapons. Once it got quiet again, I cracked the door to peep out. But as soon as I pushed the door past the threshold, gunfire opened up into the house. I screamed as I got as flat as possible on the floor of the closet. My face buried in a pair of Mr. France's stinky shoes. It had gotten dusty as the walls began to fill with holes. I could hear glass breaking and debris falling as the gunshots pierced the tiny house. Once the men stopped shooting, they waited a moment for the dust to settle down. Inside, Gordon and the France's all gathered us up to check on our well-being. The man leading the group trying to kill us ordered his men to surround the house. Twelve gunmen picked a position around the home. Once they were in place, the leader gave the kill order. The team of hitmen ran into the house. From the front to the back, they burst through windows and all doors to get in.

"Finally, we can get rid of these nuisances." The leader said to his team. He stood in the road with his arms crossed as he watched his squad invade the house.

"Sir, we do not have them." A man came in over the radio. "I repeat, we do not have them."

"What the hell are you talking about? They must be in there!" He yelled into the radio that he took from a man standing next to him.

"Sir, we checked the entire house. They are not here!"

"Amateurs!" He yelled as he slammed the radio into the man's chest next to him before walking to the house. He stepped inside and checked every room himself, pushing the soldiers out of the way.

"I'll be damned!" He screamed into the face of a nearby soldier. "Where the hell are they?!"

"They may have escaped out the back during the gunfire, Sir." One soldier spoke up and said to the irate man.

"Then go and get them, you nitwit!" He demanded the soldiers move out and search for us. "I want their bodies cold! Or, I'll happily take your useless bodies instead!"

The soldiers left the house, and the man walked out front to get back into a fancy, black SUV. His driver looked back over his shoulder at the brown-haired man.

"Where to, Mr. Maxwell?" The driver asked.

"You know what, Claudius? I think I'll just have you take me around town today," he said to the older gentleman.

"As you wish, Sir. But, anywhere, in particular, you want me to visit, Sir?"

"I always wanted to see a morgue, you?" Jacob Maxwell asked as he held a gun up to his driver.

"Yes, sir."

CHAPTER XIX

It's sickening. Nobody would have guessed this would happen in our country. So many have expressed to me that the world couldn't possibly be this corrupt. But according to the words of Waddell, power could make a man do the unthinkable.

Mr. Wesley sat in The Oval Office on this hectic day, alone. He looked through file after file of evidence from the Primotech case. His eyes watered as he faced the reality of what was being done in the shadows of industry. His cherished dream to take care of the American people had now been Withd with an insatiable need to bring them justice. He had gotten word that contacts on the ground in Idaho and other states were all dead. Communications from phones were all on an isolated grid as well as internet access. It was a lot of work to cover up a conspiracy this big. He knew of only one person who had the power to make a play on this scale.

One folder on his desk that he dreaded to open continued to catch his eye as he shuffled through the evidence. It was thick and filled to the brim with case reports. He finally opened it to look inside. Immediately stunned by what he saw, our president became angry. Each file in the folder was a person. Each exposed to the energy known as kaitrons and contracted the Codex Virus. These people were all reported to be incoherent but ready to kill everything around them.

Furthermore, most of the people were developing super strength. If there were people like this popping up everywhere, it made sense to isolate them. But Wesley couldn't agree to exterminating them.

"Mr. President, are you ready?" A secretary entered the Oval Office to ask.

"In a moment," he said to her as he closed the folder in front of him. "I just needed to view these before I spoke today."

Suddenly, his Chief of Staff burst through the door and stormed over to his desk, anger showing through the redness in his cheeks.

"You can't be serious, Mr. President, sir!" He yelled.

"You want to bet on that?" he responded as he stood up from his chair, handling his tailored suit jacket. "I cannot... I will not allow the American people to be involved in this. There are innocent lives that I must protect!"

"I understand that, but Mr. President, this is how it must be," Waddell said.

"Bull shit!" He aggressively yelled as he approached Waddell. "This is a complete violation of the constitution and everything this country was founded on."

"Yes, sir. What is it that you are having trouble with?"

"Are you kidding me! Some tech company does experiments on some ancient artifact and screws it up. Now people are getting slaughtered to accommodate it?"

"Yeah, that does sound bad."

"Bad? That is an understatement! I found out who's responsible, so I'll take care of this." He headed for the door.

"What are you going to do?" Waddell asked. The president turned around and looked at him intensely.

"I'm going to do the right thing. Principle or not, I hope you don't try to stand in my way."

The president left Waddell in The Oval by himself, watching him as he went. Everyone seemingly followed the Commander and Chief out of the office as he headed to the briefing room. Waddell made sure that he was alone and pulled out his phone to make a call to Vice President McTierman.

"He knows." He said.

"How much?"

"Let's just say that he is on his way to blow the lid clean off."

"Shit! This wasn't the plan!"

"What do I do? He's about to spill his guts on the podium in less than five minutes!"

"Waddell, you have to fix this, now!"

"Maybe he's right, though."

"Listen to me, in no world where he tells the truth that the American people will just roll over and accept it. Do something now! Our futures depend on it!"

"I ... I don't... I don't know what to do!" Waddell cried out.

"Stop Wesley before he makes a huge mistake!"

He paced the floor, worried that the president would tell the American people the truth they deserved. Suddenly, he put his phone to his face again. He made another phone call to end it. The phone rang once and stopped.

"Are you in position?" Waddell asked.

"I am." A deep voice responded.

"Do it." There was a pause.

"Last chance to change your mind."

"On my signal."

"As you wish."

The Gem State Siege

Waddell headed to the briefing room with phone in hand, hoping that he didn't have to execute his plan. The crowd of reporters all stood in wait with cameras and microphones ready as a sense of uneasiness filled the room. The president finally arrived with his secret servicemen and took to the podium affixed to the center of the stage.

"Mr. President! Mr. President!" Everyone called to get him to face their own cameras and microphones. They tried to ask questions, but he had not said a word. He simply stared into the faces of all the news reporters and paprazzis in wonder.

The president tried to speak, but his words were hoarse. He immediately closed his eyes and bowed his head, clearing his throat in the process. The crowd verbally questioning his defensive posture as they watched.

"During these awful times in our country, we are dealing with things that are... unspeakable." He started. Waddell's heart pounded as he watched in fear of what was happening.

"I am deeply saddened by the events that are taking place in the state of Idaho as we speak. I am not here to give you press and tell you that everything is going to be okay. There is something going on in this country."

People started talking in the crowd, wondering what he was referring to.

"I have come here today to expose the truth."

This sparked a wave of questions and camera flashes. Mr. Wesley raised his hand to get them to calm down.

Waddell didn't need the rest of the speech. He quickly slipped out of the room in fear that President Wesley would actually spill the details of his investigations. He hurried to pull a name from his contact and call the number. His heart pounded as the line rang and sweat beaded on his forehead as if he was standing in hot summer heat. The phone clicked and stopped ringing.

"Hello?" Waddell said. "I ne...nee... need you to do wha....wha...what we agreed on."

He looked into the meeting room and laid eyes on the President. The man on the other end responded.

"I understand. I just need it done... quickly!"

CHAPTER XX

We escaped the house and went into the town nearby, and stopped at a local tavern. We all went inside to hide out for a moment and catch our breath. All the adults with me held weapons, so it raised alarms when we went in.

"Hey, what the hell?!" The bartender yelled as he lifted up a shotgun of his own from behind the bar.

"Relax, Kong!" Lester yelled as he shut the double doors behind him. Frantic of the group holding the weapons, most people had all moved to one side or fled the bar altogether.

"Francie, what the hell are you doing, man?!" The bartender yelled again.

"Hey, look, man, we ran across some trouble and didn't have anywhere else to go," Lester explained.

"So you came into my establishment? Man, that's fucked up!"

"I'm sorry, Kong. But we're surrounded."

On a television behind the bar was the press conference held by the United States President. My mom squared herself in front of it to hear what he had to say about the world's current condition.

"On behalf of all major news outlets, I want to apologize for the selective teachings of these events. There are events taking place in this country right now that have are not sanctioned by the government. These attacks are an act of terrorism that has been hidden from the world for far too long. The ones responsible for this are in our sights. We are on the hunt for the individuals responsible for the Codex Virus and the Gem State Siege."

The Gem State Siege

The president continued. But the people in the tavern began to talk about the news report, and my mom looked back at her group with wide eyes. Suddenly, before she could turn all the way around to us, we heard screaming from the television. She gasped as she spun around and saw the American Seal on the wall behind the podium covered in blood. At the upper-right edge of the screen was an icon that indicated that this was a live event.

"No!" My mom yelled. Gasps and chilling sighs came from everyone inside the tavern as we all watched the screen in disbelief. People at the conference panicked as they tended to the Leader of the Free World. The camera fell to the floor, and the video feed was cut immediately. My dad walked over to my mom and tried to pull her away from the television and console her. But she kept breaking away from his grip. Suddenly, the electricity was cut in the bar, and a gunshot was heard outside. We could hear screams in the distance, and the people in the bar began to dive to the floor. My mom grabbed me and got down under a booth table. Suddenly, the doors were busted down, and we heard nothing but gunshots. My dad slid across the floor in front of us and came into the booth. While the France's were behind a heavy wooden table that they flipped over for cover. Officer Gordon did the same. They all filled the air inside the tavern with bullets. An entire firing squad stood in a row, putting holes into any and everyone they saw. Two police officers, a nuclear engineer, a housewife, and a bartender laid low with guns, ready to fight back from this side.

My mom stuffed me into the corner, underneath the bench, and tried to head out into the open gunfire. My dad grabbed her arm and yanked her back.

"Are you insane?! What are you doing?" He yelled.

"If we sit, we die, if we fight, we die! I've made my choice!" My mom yelled back. Suddenly the gunfire had paused for a moment, and everything went quiet. A glass fell in the aftermath, causing the squad to shoot into the direction of the bar. Gordon took notice of this occurrence and formulated a plan on the spot. He saw a broken piece of wood from a barstool nearby and reached out to grab it. Once again, the shooting stopped. He used gestures to get everyone involved in the plan and made them follow the stick with their eyes. The men all started to come deeper into the bar as they looked around for survivors. Gordon flung the piece of wood over to the wall in a dark corner, and instinctively, the men shot into the shadows. Gordon and the others jumped up from behind the table and began to ambush them. Out of six, they had killed four. The last two men fled the building and ran down the road.

"Tawnie, stay here!" Lester yelled as he and the others ran after the men. The group ran down the road, shooting at the fleeing soldiers as the predator became the prey. My mom and I held on to one another. I could feel her trembling in fear as I peeped out into the room to see if anyone was still there. She pulled me back and slid out into the open to check the bodies of the fallen soldiers.

"Mommy!" I called out to her.

"Wait here, Milo. I'll be back."

I stayed under the table and watched my mom as she tip-toed over to the bodies of the fallen soldiers. She took a knee next to one of them and began to pull things from his armor. She thought she may need some of the items in the future. But, there was one issue. One of the soldiers was very much alive.

"Mom!" I called out. "Behind you!" My mom turned

The Gem State Siege

around in time to avoid a knife that was only centimeters away from piercing her skin. She stumbled backward as she tripped over the dead body behind her.

"Hey, wait!" She pleaded as she held her hands up, trying to get away from the soldier. "You don't have to do this!"

My mother knew that she was on her own and that there was nobody here to save her. But she was more concerned about me than herself at that moment. The man stood there with the knife pointed at her, eyes locked into hers. Suddenly, he noticed the gun on the floor and stared at it.

"Sir, please." My mom said to him once more. "I am just a little unarmed woman. You couldn't possibly be that heartless as to kill me this way, not in front of my five-year-old son. I stepped out of the shadows and walked over to my mother, not knowing how much more dangerous I made the situation.

"No, no, no!" She said to me. "Milo, no, stay there, Sweetie!" The man looked over at me with the coldest of looks in his eyes. I could still see the horror in his mind through his expression, even silhouetted by the daylight.

"Mommy," I called out with tears in my eyes as I took small steps backward.

"Don't you dare hurt him!" My mother screamed as she stepped closer to the man. He looked back down at the gun again and put the knife in his pocket. He bent over to pick up the gun, and my mom ran to kick him in the back of the knee. This took the soldier down, and she went to grab the weapon, but the man was faster in capturing it. She tried to wrestle the gun away from him, but he took the opportunity to elbow her in the mouth. As she almost lost consciousness, she still fought to take the rifle from the man's hands. Eventually, he was able to shake her off. This prompted an opportunity for him to attack her. Her bruised ribs from the night before made it almost impossible for her to fight back. She was thrown into the table by the booth that she told me to hide in.

"Mommy, get up!" I screamed as she laid in front of me, writhing in pain. But despite the discomfort, she still jumped back up to defend me. The soldier took a few steps towards us, and my mother went to stand in front of me and held her arms out.

"Please, don't do this!" She screamed again. But the man lifted the barrel of his rifle and pointed it at her chest. There was a cold, ominous wind blowing through the tavern as my mother stood before the soldier. She hoped that at some point before the shot was fired that someone in her group would intervene. But nobody came.

"Please... Just.." My mom said as she got choked up. "All I ask is that you spare my son." But again, the man said nothing.

But suddenly, she performed one final gambit, and it made the difference. The sound of the gunshot pierced the silence in the little town. My eyes were closed as it happened, so I didn't see it. I experienced a flash of light, followed by a short wave of heat, and assumed it was the gun's muzzle flash. I felt my mom stumble and believed that she had been shot.

"Mommy!" I screamed as I looked up at her, noticing that something was not right. She stood there, solid and staring at the man who was now wavering in his stance. He dropped the rifle and fell to the ground. My mother fell to her knees and watched her hand.

"Mommy, are you okay?" I asked. But she did not answer. I took the opportunity to look at her hands and saw the most magnificent sight that I had ever seen. Her fingertips were glowing, and the light was expelled from the inside of her hands.

My mom stood back up and walked over to the man's body.

"Milo." She called out to me. I hurried over to her. As I looked down at him, I noticed that he had a gaping hole through his chest. His heart blasted entirely out of his body, and the spot was singed. There was no blood coming from his body. I looked back up at my mom, and the look on her face was just as cold as the look of the gunman when he looked at me.

"Mommy?" I called out to her.

"I'm okay, Milo. We're okay."

In the silence, I could hear static as we began to leave the tavern. My mom pulled out a radio that she confiscated from the dead soldier.

"Someone on this damn line better tell me that they found my package!" A man yelled.

"Sir, we have a location of the package and are sending in reinforcements to get it."

"What the hell? Who stole it?" He asked.

"We have yet to uncover that information, sir."

"Get that package back and get back to the lab!"

"On it, Mr. Maxwell."

She put down the radio, and I could see the anger form in her eyes. Once she heard that name, it made her face twitch. For some reason, that name rang to her, and she was now angrier than ever.

CHAPTER XXI

A few minutes later, the others came back to the tavern looking for us.

"Tawnie!" I could hear my dad yelling as they came running down the street. "Milo!"

"Daddy!" I called out to him. "We're here!"

I left the booth that I was sitting in and ran over to the door, dodging debris with each step. My mom was still on her knees, taking merchandise from the soldiers' bodies. My dad ran in, and I immediately jumped into his arms as he entered the room.

"Oh, thank goodness!" He said as he kissed my forehead. He then looked over at my mother, her eyes locked on him as she stuffed ammo magazines into her backpack. Close behind were the other adults coming back into the tavern.

"Did you guys find them?" She asked.

"We did," Gordon answered.

As Gordon made his way over to my mother, he saw the body with the gaping hole through the chest. He took a knee to get a closer look at the wound and raised an eyebrow.

"What the hell happened to this guy?" He asked my mom. She then gave me a look that suggested I stay quiet. I was on the receiving end of this look from her many times throughout my life.

"He got back up after you guys left, and I had to put him down." My mom said.

"With what, a cannon?"

"I defended my child. That's all that matters."

"Are you okay?" My dad asked her as he extended his hand to help her up. Instead of accepting the gesture, she stood up on her own, making eye contact with him the entire time. I had no idea how bad the relationship between my parents was at the time. It wouldn't be until much later in life that I understood why my mom was so frustrated with him. My dad looked at her as she walked past him. She gave a spiteful scowl that one would only deliver to the bitterest of enemies.

"What the hell is your problem?!" my dad yelled at her. My mother stopped walking, took a deep breath, and closed her eyes. The others all stood in shock at how my dad chose to handle the problem.

"I think we are just going to... Find something over there?" Lester suggested to his wife.

"Oh yeah, good idea, honey!" She responded. "We have to go do a thing." The two of them took the hostile opportunity to leave while still peeping back at the arguing couple.

Gordon shook his head and did the same. He stopped at the door and looked back to me over his shoulder.

"Milo." He called me. Confused, I looked up at my parents for confirmation. My mom still had her eyes closed as tears ran down her face. My dad continued to stare a hole into her as his face turned a burning shade of red.

"Mommy?" I called out, hoping for a bit of direction.

"Go, Milo." She softly said to me with a cracking voice. Reluctantly, I left the tavern with Officer Gordon, and we headed up the street to meet with the others.

"Hey there, Little Man!" Victoria said as she squatted to get at eye level with me. I was startled as I was too busy focusing on my parents. She ignored my frustrations and began to do her best to make me feel comfortable. She started to tickle me, and I laughed at her efforts to cheer me up until my anger got the best of me. As my fist swung up to hit the woman, she caught my hand and began to squeeze. It was not tight enough to hurt me, but definitely enough to startle me and send a message. I looked into her eyes as she grew more serious by the second.

"A great warrior always manages his anger during conflict." She said to me.

I pulled my hand back and stepped away.

"Milo." Officer Gordon called out. I looked up at him, blinded by the sun as it beamed from behind him.

"Everything will be fine. I promise." He smiled at me.

Back at the tavern, my mom and dad stared at one another for a moment. Anticipating the argument they were about to have, they dreaded the words that needed to be said. For they knew how dangerous it could be to their relationship.

"I know you're mad, but I believe we can fix this, Tawnie." Were my dad's first words.

"No, it's too late!" She screamed at him. "Do you understand what you did? Have you any idea what you helped unleash on our society?" My dad was silent. His head held low, he had no choice but to take my mother's words as he knew it to be futile to respond.

"I... I just—"

"You just what? How many times did I warn you of the dangers of working for this company?"

"Many times before. But I didn't listen."

"Oh, now you want to agree?" She yelled as she stepped closer to him. "Over and over, no matter how many times I warned, time and time again. What did it take for you to realize that I was right, Milo?"

Still, he had no words. He stared in anguish as he waited for her to finish.

The Gem State Siege

"Answer me!"
"I can't."

She chuckled as she turned to leave the wrecked establishment.

"All it took was the collapse of a government and a coalition that believes that we are better off dead. These were the circumstances that caused you to finally believe what I was telling you all along."

"What did you expect me to do!?" He screamed at her. "How was I supposed to know this would be how it turned out?"

"Milo." My mother called out to him. "Your job was to make sure it turned out this way. And the kicker is, you could have stopped it long ago."

"I could have been dead already, Tawnie." He argued. My mother took a deep breath and turned back to face him.

"Now, he's too strong to stop, Milo." She said.

"Maxwell?"

"Had I known that you were playing both sides, I could have handled this myself."

Tears ran down my mother's face as she did her best to remain non-violent in the situation.

"No, you couldn't do—" My mom cut him off with a raised hand.

"I am complete on my own, Milo. You do not tell me what to do."

"What do you think you're going to do? It's not like you have an army of men ready to go to war for you."

She stopped to think about what my dad said and walked toward the exit again.

"You have helped to create a world where I am not

The Gem State Siege

allowed to exist, and I can't be a part of it anymore." She said to him.

"Wait, are you talking about the gender equality thing that I slipped up and said before? And what world can't you exist in?" My dad asked with a smile on his face as he ran around to cut her off. "It wasn't that serious, and can you calm down, please?"

"I'm calmer than I've ever been before, Milo."

My dad tried to step forward and reach for her face, but she stepped backward to evade him.

"Tawnie."

"There is no other way. This is how it has to be."

"What are you talking about?" He screamed, frustrated that the conversation was not going his way. "We can drop this thing in a volcano and just go hide somewhere tropical. That way, nobody gets their hands on it."

"Because I am part of the problem, and I don't get the option to just flee at first sight of uncertainty."

My dad reached out to grab her arm and pulled her close. But my mother broke away from him as her hand began to glow. She held her palm to my father's face as she silently threatened to take him down.

His eyes grew wide as he stared into the light with amazement and fear. The heat was so intense that he had to step away.

"You're one of them." He said to her as he began to smile. "Do you know what this means?"

"I do." My mother said to him.

"This is an astounding breakthrough for science." He added with a hint of joy. My mother then let her anger get the best of her. She whipped her arm out to the side and sent a wave of light straight from her hand. The beam blasted through the wall and went to the building on the opposite side of the street. Their eyes still locked, she made it a point to let him know that she was actually done with their relationship.

"I'll do my best to protect our son from this world that you created, but I don't want you anywhere near him!" My mom left him standing in the tavern by himself as he had no choice but to watch her walk away. She reached down into her pocket as she walked up the road and pulled out the Pyro Stone. That was the moment that my father realized that he no longer had it.

CHAPTER XXII

My mother came back to find us up the road. Noticing that she was alone, I immediately wondered where my dad was. When I asked, she took a knee in front of me and wrapped her arms around me.

"Mommy loves you. You know that, right?" She said to me.

"Yeah," I responded. She then kissed me on the forehead. I could remember feeling how cold her lips were as they touched my face, and I felt an uneasiness. I knew something was wrong.

"I want my daddy," I whined as she stood.

"Where is Senior?" Lester asked my mom.

"I left him." She said as she walked through the group, pulling me along with her. Victoria looked at Officer Gordon with a suggestive eye. Gordon shook his head and began to walk after her.

"Did something happen?" Victoria asked.

"Yes, I am not respected in my relationship, nor am I treated fairly." She stated. "I gave 12 years to that genius-level idiot, and he screws me far too often. And not even in the good, fun kind."

"What exactly are you talking about?" Asked Lester.

My mom stopped walking. She stood silent for a moment. They all looked around at one another as they waited for her to respond. When she turned to the group, she looked at them with concern in her eyes.

"I don't know if I like that look," Gordon said to her.

"Yeah, me neither." She responded.

"What's going on, Tawnie?" Yet again, she stalled as her

head fell. It appeared as if she was thinking, but when I looked up, I could see something in her eyes that I didn't usually see... hatred.

"I'm just worn out because of everything that's happening, is all."

"No. Try again," Gordon said to her as he stepped closer.

"Guys, I don't know how to say it... but." She trailed off.

"Bad news about our current position?" Lester asked.

"No, this is something else," Gordon said to him.

"Look, you need to stop acting like you know me!" She exploded.

"If you are to be a psychiatrist in America, you will know how it feels to be analyzed yourself."

"I am tired of you men always trying to lord your dominance over me! I'm sick of it!"

"What the hell is your problem? Did I do something to you?" He asked as he turned his hand to himself in question. She then took a deep breath and turned away from the group.

As my mother walked away, Gordon ran around us and cut her off.

"Oh no, you don't!" He said with his palm up to her. "We do not have the time for petty issues and temper tantrums. Your problems with you and your husband will stay between you and your husband and will be revisited after we are not on the brink of death!"

Tears formed in her eyes. She looked at him as if a parent was scolding his child.

"Do I make myself clear?" He asked. With no words, my mother nodded her head.

"Don't talk to my mommy like that!" I yelled at him as I stood in front of her, so-called defending her honor.

"Milo!" She called out to me as she yanked my collar.

The Gem State Siege

"My daddy will get you!" I ignorantly told him.

The stone-cold man got down to eye level with me and looked at me with the coldest of looks.

"Young man, you will learn that it's the heroes that you will have to watch the closest in life." He glanced at my mom.

"Where is your husband, Tawnie?" Lester asked.

"I left him in the tavern." She answered.

"Should we go get him?"

"He is a traitor. I don't see the benefit of aligning myself with someone like him."

I looked up at my mom with horror as she concluded her sentence. How dare she say something like that about my father, I thought. What happened between them? Luckily, I wasn't the only one asking that question. The more she was asked, the more my mother evaded the truth. Lester asked again, but she dodged the question a second time.

"Where is Milo?" They asked.

"I said, he's in the tavern!" She responded.

"Why did you leave him there?"

"Can we go?" I watched my mom dance around the truth, all for not showing her emotions in front of the others.

They all stood silent and stared at her with impatience etched in their expressions. My mother waited for them to keep asking, but they were done. Thinking back to the conversation she had with my father, she got emotional all over.

"Let it out," Gordon said as he approached her. He put his arms around her, and she immediately began to sob against his chest. The look on Gordon's face was a look of hurt as he waited for her to finish. He didn't rush her grieving at all, however. Despite being in a partial war zone, nobody said a thing.

I looked up at my mother and saw tears that poured from her eyes during the situation. All I could do was stand and wait, and I didn't want to be the one to interrupt. But eventually, she was back to normal.

"I don't have time to fill you guys in now." She said while wiping her face. "What do we do?" She asked Gordon.

"We get out of this city before they come for us." He said.

"We seem to have halted their plans to storm Rexburg. But it's only a matter of time before they come with reinforcements."

"Right," Lester said. "But where do we go from here?"

Gordon paused for a moment and looked around at them, unsure if he could continue.

"Gordon, what is it?" Mom asked.

"I'm not sure if we could go to them. They are not supposed to exist in the public eye."

"Who?" Lester asked as he turned his head to the side in confusion.

"Danny, you don't mean..." Victoria started to say with looks of suggestion to him. He nodded his head in uncertainty.

"It could be the only way."

Victoria stared at Gordon for a moment, and it raised more concern to Lester.

"What's going on here?" He asked his wife.

"There is an organization that tried to recruit us while we were still enlisted. They looked like and operated like the government, but there is no information on them." Victoria explained. "Danny, how do we know this isn't them?"

"It's not." He sternly responded.

"How do we know it isn't?"

"Any group that devotes themselves to destroying evidence of events like this wouldn't pop out and start killing people."

"Who is this organization? "My mother asked.

"I'm not sure." He answered. "I have a card from a man named Toreon Kane. But, I'm pretty sure that Happy House Inc. Is just a codename."

"Kane?" My mom repeated.

"You know him?" Victoria asked.

"His name sure as hell does sound familiar. But Happy House Inc. is definitely not ringing a bell."

"Got it. The card says they are located in Jackpot, Nevada." Gordon added.

"Jackpot? That's over two-hundred miles away from here!" Victoria said.

"Well, I guess we'll need to get moving then," Gordon said.

My mom began to walk down the road with me at her side.

"Tawnie!" Victoria called out to her. My mom turned around to acknowledge her. But upon seeing the look of concern on everyone's face, she became puzzled. She then approached the group again, knowing exactly what they were thinking about.

"What is it, guys?" She asked.

"Are you certain you want to leave your husband behind?" Lester asked. "He may have done wrong, but nobody deserves to be left for dead, do they?"

"No." She answered. "I just don't know how to face him

now."

"You take responsibility for your side of the conflict. Then you compromise with him for a resolution. That is what marriage is." Gordon told her.

My mother nodded and crossed her arms. Her head fell as she thought about how horrible she would feel if something happened to my dad.

"Hey!" Gordon yelled. "We're right behind you."

With a smile on her face, she turned around and began to walk towards the tavern. Like he promised, Gordon followed closely behind. Citizens rallied as they wondered what was happening in their little community. It seemed that the destroyed tavern was the focal point of everyone's attention. As we arrived, my mother ran to the bar screaming for my dad.

"Milo! Milo!" As she broke through the crowd of shocked civilians. However, she noticed the tavern was empty. My dad was gone.

"Milo? Shit!" She ran back out of the building through the crowd of bystanders gawking at the dead bodies.

Once she returned to us, she looked around the city street for clues about where my father went.

"Where could he have possibly gone?" My mom asked as she diligently looked around for him. Suddenly, I spotted a black SUV, just like the one we were in, sitting on the road in the distance.

"Mommy!" I called out as I pointed to the vehicle. The adults all took a look at the car and gasped.

"No!" My mom yelled. But, Gordon and Lester both dashed off towards the vehicle. Unfortunately, it began to leave as they were getting closer. Gordon looked back at my mother in shock as the two of them began to speculate that my dad was actually inside.

CHAPTER XXIII

Terrifying is the only way to describe the time that changed the entire course of reality. While we fought for our lives in Rexburg, a meeting took place in Arlington, Virginia, to discuss what happens to our country next. The Vice President of the United States rallied for the safety of the public. The problem was, there were terrified people throughout the nation. This included ones who helped make decisions. Here is what I learned about fear on this day. Man will do anything and everything in his power to be rational, except for when it comes to fear. I didn't hear this conversation personally. But from what I hear, the government could have easily prevented this reckoning. But biases and personal agendas also played a part in the problem. Our vice president, Hawthorne McTierman, sat in a room with the entire White House staff and presidential party. This was when they came up with the bright idea to make this guy the new acting president. I will reserve my personal issues with McTierman for the moment.

"Mr. Vice President, what are we doing in light of this situation?" A senator asked.
"We have a special task force in the state of Idaho and surrounding borders who are containing the Codex as we speak." He answered with confidence.
"What exactly is this Codex Virus?" Another asked.
"It was explained to me to be an unfortunate side effect of a recently funded experiment."
"Who conducted this said experiment, And how did it end up getting out?"
"That is something that I am not knowledgeable on now.

Yet, we are taking measures to defend ourselves against the virus."

They all looked at one another in suspicion of what the Vice President said.

"How do we defend ourselves against a top-secret virus that we do not know anything about?" The Congressman asked. "And are we certain this is the disease that is causing our meta-human problem in America?"

The Vice President sat to ponder the statement and looked down at the notes in front of him.

"Gentlemen!" Waddell yelled. "The Vice President is not at liberty to answer any of your questions right now."

"The only thing we should be focused on is the man who assassinated our President." The Vice President added.

"Have we found him yet, Mr. Wallace?" He asked the Secretary of Defense George Wallace.

"There have been no updates on the perpetrator at this time. He is still at large."

"We pay a lot of money for our resources. I suggest you use them!" Waddell yelled. Wallace just shook his head.

"You know, you've gotten soft in your day." He said back to Wallace. The two of them began to chuckle.

"I'm not sure that I could stand behind the goal of keeping the people in the dark like this, Mr. Vice President." The Senator said. "As all this is exposed, shouldn't we be informing the public of this?"

"Absolutely not." Said Waddell.

"The less the people know, the easier it will be to clean up the aftermath when this is over," McTierman responded.

"They have a right to know if they are exposed to a deadly illness, Mr. Vice President."

"Senator, trust me, the Codex could be a slight inconvenience for those that contract it. But it is only dangerous to those that don't get it."

"In conclusion, Gentlemen, The Vice President is a busy man and has to go tend to other important matters. So if you'd excuse us."

The others left the room with more questions than answers. But the Vice President didn't want to sacrifice his transition into presidency.

"You think it worked?" McTierman asked as the door closed behind the other men.

"I think we successfully bought you some time," Waddell answered.

"How are we really doing out there in those states?"

Waddell took a moment to sigh as he sat across from McTierman at the table and looked him square in the eyes.

"Now, why would you concern yourself with something so trivial?" He chuckled. "You and I both know that your time would be better suited by—"

"Allan!" McTierman cut him off. The two men stared at one another intently. Waddell was shocked that the Vice President was actually upset about this issue.

"Sir..." Waddell stammered. "The entire state of Idaho has been infected with the Codex Virus."

"What are we doing to contain it?"

"Mr. Vice President, you do not want to go down that rabbit hole. I promise—"

"Who is in charge of the recon mission?" He asked, cutting Waddell off again

"Jacob Maxwell, sir."

All of a sudden, McTierman looked as if he had seen a ghost.

The Gem State Siege

"What have we done?"

CHAPTER XXIV

Back in Rexburg, our group traveled through the city with haste as we attempted to head in the same direction as the black SUV. The more we ran, the more it seemed we would never get to where we were going. Which, by the way, we had no idea where "there" was. The streets were almost empty despite the weather bringing a day with clear skies. The sun was setting, and my mom began to fear that we were already too late. She ran out in front of the group, trying to look around for any signs that my dad was nearby.

"Milo!" She called out over and over, hoping that my dad would somehow miraculously pop up somewhere.

Suddenly, she tripped up from exhaustion and fell to her knees. All the others ran over to check on her. I walked with Victoria to allow my mother to go ahead. But it seemed like she was running on empty at this point. I could see Gordon and Lester tending to her and help her back to her feet. But she swiped at them as she began to cry.

"Dammit!" She screamed with tears in her eyes. Victoria and I had caught up to them, and my mother was still hysterical at my father's kidnapping.

"Mommy?" I called out.

"Tawnie, we will find those scumbags and get him back," Gordon said to her. But my mother stayed on her knees and never looked up. Every few seconds, she would sniffle, indicating that she was still crying. Her hair had fallen over her face, so I couldn't see her eyes, but it seemed that she was now in that dark space again. I was forced to watch what I know now to be an internal struggle that none of us could see then.

The Gem State Siege

"Where could they have taken him?" Victoria asked.

"Not sure," Gordon said as he still focused on my mother. He stayed by her side and rubbed her back as she struggled to pull herself together.

"Maybe they have a hideout here somewhere... But—" Lester started to say.

"Goddammit! What do these people want?" Victoria cried out. I let go of Victoria's hand and walked over to my mother.

"Mommy?" I timidly called out to her. When she lifted her head, I could see something in her eyes that I had never seen before. But I ignored it, thinking that she was just upset at the situation. I stepped forward and wrapped my arms around her. To my surprise, she did not reciprocate the gesture. I found this odd, but once again, I ignored it. When I pulled myself back, she just stared at me with a look that I could not interpret at all at the moment. At the age of five, not understanding what was going on, it was challenging to keep up with these issues. I speculate that in my life now, I have figured out what that look meant. But in this story, it's not relevant.

"Gordon, what do we do now?" Victoria asked.

"We keep looking. We have to find him." He said. "Tawnie, can you continue?"

Unfortunately, my mother was so out of it that she could not answer. She just stared at me with a deranged look on her face.

"Mommy, what's wrong?" I asked her as I yanked her arm. Suddenly, I was pushed back by Gordon, who bent over to pick my mom up by her armpits.

"Snap out of it!" He yelled at her. "Now is not the time for you to be breaking down!"

My mom looked at him with disdain as he hoisted her up

above his head. Suddenly, she snapped back into reality and screamed back at him to put her down. Gordon threw my tiny mother, and she landed on her feet but stumbled a bit before regaining her composure.

He shook his head at her. The other two were baffled at what happened.

"Tawnie, are you okay?" Victoria asked. My mom looked at her nonchalantly, making the woman uncomfortable.

"I'm as good as a woman could be in this situation." She answered.

"It seemed like we lost you just now. That was the only reason I asked."

"Lost me how?" My mother questioned her.

"It looked like you were lost in your own head. Do you remember what happened just now?"

"Yes!" My mom exploded. "We're looking for the good-for-nothing idiots that kidnapped my husband!" She said with tears in her eyes.

"We have definitely seen this behavior before," Gordon said as he stared at my mom.

"Yeah," Victoria said. "Anyone who was ever deployed knows what that is."

"Guys." Lester tried to interrupt the conversation. His wife and friend ignored him as he stared off into the distance. I tried to see what was interesting about the horizon, but I could not see anything. Back and forth conversations dominated the group until finally, Lester yelled to shut them up. The three of them looked at him in wonder.

"What the hell?" Victoria asked.

"You guys don't see that?" He asked, looking into the endless fields outside the city. The others, including my mother, looked out into the distance with him.

The Gem State Siege

"What are we supposed to be seeing?" Gordon asked as he focused on the scenery. "Wait."

"Is that a—" Victoria started to say.

"You have got to be kidding me!" My mother exploded.

Just outside the city, about a mile into the fields, there was a vehicle posted there. Not far from that one, another one sat. And at the road leading into town, there was another road check set up. The entire city was now under siege. We could see the shadows of soldiers and their black SUVs in the distance in every direction we looked. My mother sat down on the ground and just gazed. At that moment, the look from earlier returned. She went silent, and all the adults realized that she had slipped into a different zone again.

The moment went by like the world was going in slow motion around us. As my mother realized the danger we were in, she jumped up from the ground and grabbed me. Gunshots echoed through the land as the adults ran for solace. We entered a nearby alleyway and hid out for a moment. The gunshots had stopped, and it had gotten quiet again. As we waited, some civilians occasionally entered the snipers' scopes. They were immediately picked off with no remorse. The haunting sight of heads exploding as they tried to make it through the streets will always stay with me.

"We have to get away from the outskirts!" Gordon said to us.

"Remember, boys, not unless they cross the line. Don't have too much fun." We all heard coming from my mother's direction. The other adults looked at her with concern.

"What the hell was that?" Lester asked.

"Do you have one of their radios?" Gordon asked. As she tried to stay calm by breathing deeply, she nodded her head.

Being the closest to the corner of the building, my mom looked around it. Suddenly, without warning, she walked out into the open. We all yelled out to her as she foolishly walked out from behind cover. Gordon ran out to grab her, but she simply held her hand out to signal him to stop. She stood still with her head held low. Gordon was astonished after realizing what she saw.

"No way," Victoria said. The group of mercenaries had boxed us all inside the city. A single white line had been painted on the ground and seemed to span as far as we could see. We could hear footsteps approaching from behind us, so we all turned to look. A young man ran over to us, frantic about what was happening, but my mother still faced the siege in the distance.

"What the hell is wrong with the world?" The panicked young man screamed as he ran past my mother.

"No, wait!" She yelled as she reached out to grab him.

"Pow!" A single shot echoed. It was too late. Blood splattered all over us, and a headless body toppled over just inches away from where we stood. We all jumped back from the line for our own safety. My mother turned away and stepped over to me to wipe the blood from my eyes and face. Gordon stepped forward with anger in his eyes. He began to grind his teeth as he contemplated something drastic.

"Danny, no!" Victoria yelled at him as she urged everyone to step away from the line. Angry, Lester and Gordon stepped back with pure rage in their eyes. Once it became clear that we were not leaving or finding my father, we all bit the bullet and headed back into town.

CHAPTER XXV

When night fell, we headed to the only spot where there was light. As the sun set, the temperature dropped, and the crisp winter air began to sweep the city. Still, without power, the need to light bonfires became evident as many places were illuminated in the dark night. We chose a spot where many people gathered and invited ourselves to the heat of the flames. My mother took off her backpack and opened it, remembering that she had a jacket for me to wear. As she pulled it out, the Pyro Stone illuminated from her leather sack. But she hurried to stuff it back down so that nobody saw it.

As she placed my arms into the jacket's sleeves, Gordon and Lester started to notice dirty looks from the locals.

"We don't want any trouble, sir," Victoria said to a man sitting near us. He angrily looked at us as he held his hands out for warmth from the heat.

"You don't look like you're from around here!" the old man yelled at us. Immediately, my mother's head snapped in his direction. Gordon held his arm out in front of her to assure that she would not cause an uproar. But immediately, she pushed his arm out of the way.

"Sir, we are here in the cold, just like you, trapped by juiced-up lunatics." She said to him. "All I want to do is get my kid some heat so that I can be free to figure out a plan. With that being said, I suggest you shut up before you end up making out with these embers. Or walk away and hope I don't shoot you in the back of the neck!"

Everyone became aware of us and turned their attention to our little group. The man stood up and walked away. Just as

The Gem State Siege

he left the bench, an older woman walked past him, tapping his shoulder as she approached to sit at the bonfire with us.

"Your friend is a little abrasive, huh?" The elder, white-haired woman asked.

"I don't speak for her, ma'am," Gordon said.

"Hmm. My apologies. I'm hardly ever wrong about that stuff." She said as she cackled. Everyone looked around at one another as the confusion started to kick in. I could feel my mother tense up behind me as she grew suspicious of the woman.

"You'd have to excuse Tarker." The woman said. "He is defensive of territories for some reason."

"Like we told him, we don't want any trouble," Gordon reassured.

"Me neither." She stated as she stared into the flames with fear on her face.

"But you people are from out of town. Are the other areas in the state as bad as this right now?"

"Worse. Everyone is dead on the way here from the south." My mother answered. The old woman shook her head at the news.

"What are they here for?"

"They are here to get the Pyro Stone." My mom said without caution.

"The Pyro Stone?" The woman yelled. "That cannot be! It can't be here in Rexburg."

"Ma'am, what do you know about the Pyro Stone," Gordon asked. The woman began to look around at our environment to see if anyone was close enough to hear our conversation."

"Believe what you want to believe, but it is said that The Pyro Stone was created by God himself." My mother began to giggle as she looked away.

The Gem State Siege

"Something funny, child?"

"Yeah, the stone is not made by mythical beings from outer space." My mom laughed.

"Careful, you are in Mormon Territory!"

"Ma'am!" My mother yelled at the woman. Startled, she just stared at my mom with wide eyes. After a few seconds of an awkward stare-off, the woman got up and walked away.

Gordon and the France's all stared at my mother.

"What?" She asked, shrugging her shoulders with a hint of attitude.

"Do you have to be so rude?" Victoria asked. "I mean, seriously, Tawnie. We have enemies out there. Let us be in peace for a moment at least."

"I'm sorry, guys." My mom said as she dropped her head.

"We'll get him back," Gordon said to her. My mom looked down again, clutching her arms around me.

"Is that what's on your mind?"

"In part." She said.

"What is the other part?"

"This entire situation. Had we not been involved in Maxwell's plans, we would all be better off. So many people wouldn't have to die."

"No, you don't know that," Lester said. "And it isn't like any of us had a choice."

"He's right. We all chose life in the heat of a moment in time. Anyone else would have made the same decision." Victoria added.

My mother jumped up from the bench and paced in front of us.

"Guys, those are excuses!" She yelled. "If it weren't for you two being a part of the archeology crew, Milo wouldn't have needed a police escort. Then, they wouldn't have fallen onto my radar when I blasted them on my platform. We were all part of a chain of events that is about to get everyone killed."

"I just want to say that if it weren't us, someone else would have done it," Lester added. The other two nodded in agreement. My mom threw her hands up to her head, full of anger.

"He has us trapped like rats in a cage, and you guys can make jokes?"

"Tawnie, relax! You are going to make these people come over here." Gordon said.

She looked at all the people as if she was developing an idea. Her eyes fluttering and her lips mouthed silent words.

"What are you thinking?" Gordon asked as he jumped up from the bench.

"We fight fire with fire." She said to him.

"Absolutely not, Tawnie!" Lester yelled as he jumped up as well. "We will not get these innocent people involved in this mess."

"These innocent people are in here with us. They are already involved." Victoria argued. My mom looked around Lester at Victoria.

"It's about time you take the woman stance."

"Well, there are dumb plans, then there are unrealistic plans." She said to my mom as she stood up. "I just know that we can't possibly do this on our own. These people deserve to have the option to die with dignity, so let's give it to them."

My mother bounced with excitement as she looked around once again.

"So, I'm assuming that we are the targets of this attack?"

Gordon asked my mom. She didn't answer him with anything more than a smirk.

"But to be fair—" She started. "Everyone here is in danger. If you guys can remember that Codex Virus that the news was referring to."

"Which would be?" Asked Lester.

"Somehow, they used the stone to create artificial serums that awaken what's called the caster gene inside the human body."

"Caster, huh?" Gordon said.

"Yeah, it's the genetic strand that allows a human to gain elemental abilities based on their genetic makeup."

"Wait, that sounds cool!" Said Lester. "So we are all infected?"

"We are, but a majority of humankind doesn't have this caster gene inside of them. The ones who don't will lose their brains' function, develop super strength, and try to kill us all. Good news, though! Nobody here has the caster gene!" My mom explained. All three of them stared at her as if she had lost her mind.

"How do you know this?" Gordon asked. My mom walked back to the bench and grabbed her backpack. She opened it and pulled out the laptop.

"It probably has a bit of juice left if you want to see the research and plans on the Siege."

"No, I trust you," Gordon said as he guided her arm down to lower the laptop.

Gordon noticed a large group of people around us, moving in a strange and unsettling way. So he spaced out of the conversation to watch.

"How could the government allow this to happen?" Victoria asked.

The Gem State Siege

"I honestly believe that the government is clear of the blame. But, Jacob Maxwell is as guilty as they come." My mother responded.

"Why do you say that?"

"Somehow, Maxwell extorted the funds for the experiment from the government. Unfortunately, they did nothing to prevent his company from experimenting with real people. This laptop holds all the evidence. Assuming we don't survive for any other reason. In that case, it would and should be to expose Maxwell for attempting to singlehandedly destroy the world."

"Sounds like you got this all planned out," Gordon said to her.

"I had to. If not, that monster will get what he wants, Gordon. Once we get Milo back, we need to kill him."

My mom noticed Gordon's sense of discomfort as his eyes continued to cut from side to side.

"What's wrong?" She asked him. Suddenly, Lester and Victoria stood up and looked around as well. Stepping towards us from the shadows was Tarker, the man from before. He stood with a few guys who all had weapons in their hands. In a matter of seconds, we had become surrounded by townspeople. All because of my mother's temper, they all wished to do us harm.

CHAPTER XXVI

"Tawnie. See what you did?" Lester asked.
"Apparently, you hurt some feelings," Victoria announced.
The townspeople closed in on us, giving death glares.
"Mommy!" I called out as I grabbed hold of her leg and squeezed tight.
"Milo, relax! We're going to be fine."

Tarker approached us with a steel baseball bat in his hand.
"Wait, Tarker, is it?" She asked him. "Are you willing to beat down a young grieving widow just to prove a point?"
"I am willing to make an example of you for being disrespectful." He seethed.
"I don't think you understand."
"No?" He said as he approached us. "We can't let an outsider come into our town and disrespect anyone here."

My mother laughed as she stepped around the man to grab the laptop. As she walked past him, the street thug raised his bat to block my mom's path.
"Man or woman, you will pay the price."
"This is not going to go the way you think." She said as she moved the bat aside with her index finger.
"Oh yeah?" The man said to her. "And why is that? Is pretty boy over there gonna make a move?" He said as he walked over to look Gordon in the eyes. He stood there for a moment, and the two men went silent. Tarker jumped at Gordon, but the hardened police officer did not flinch.
"Oh, tough guy, huh?" He asked.
"Well, he probably arrested idiots like you every day."

My mom joked.

"Who are you calling an idiot, lady! Do you know I will take you out in front of your son?"

"You will not!" She yelled back at him as she swung her backpack over her shoulder. "You actually need us."

"And why would I need a little pipsqueak like you?" He asked.

"If you actually want to leave this place alive, then you are going to need my guidance. And I am going to need your strength."

"Wait?" Gordon asked. "Did you orchestrate this entire scenario?"

My mother smirked in a devious manner as she floated to the top of the bench next to us.

"Alright, ladies and gentlemen. Rexburg is quarantined due to a made-up virus that I'm sure all of us have. So inherently, we're all dangerous." She announced. The crowd began to talk among each other as hissing from whispers filled the air.

"What do you mean we are dangerous?" The elderly woman asked.

"Apparently, the Codex Virus gives people special abilities and powers."

"What the hell?" One citizen asked. "That doesn't even remotely make sense."

"Right!" Another man called out. "You are a nut case!"

"A virus that gives you powers?" Another woman laughed.

"Think about it," my mother said as she jumped down from the bench and parted the crowd as she walked through it.

"The news said this was a pandemic. Which we have had

before. Never before has there been a lockdown that involves guns and on-site eliminations. This is not a mission to contain a virus for them. This a mission to exterminate us all."

"Can't they just make a vaccine for this so-called virus?" A man asked from a distance.

"I can assure you, If Jacob Maxwell wanted to vaccinate us, he would have never put out the kill order." She announced with a smile on her face.

"Jacob Maxwell?" A few people shouted as they began to defend the maniacal entrepreneur.

"Jacob Maxwell is the most philanthropic being on this planet!"

At this point, Gordon, Lester, and Victoria took me and stood back from the mob. We all watched as my mother worked the crowd as if she was in concert. There didn't seem to be a single person uninterested in this impromptu meeting.

"Jacob Maxwell would not do something this corrupt!" A citizen yelled.

"Well, these men are all Primotech assets." My mom argued. "Look, people, you don't have to believe me. Eventually, those goons out there are going to cross the line and come into this city and kill everyone." The crowd grew silent as they started to listen.

"If we allow him to eliminate us like he did to the rest of the state—" Suddenly, the crowd talked amongst themselves and ignored her.

"Tawnie!" Gordon called out to her. My mom came over to us.

"You can't recruit innocent people to help you fight special-ops soldiers." He said.

"Gordon, what other choice do we have?" She asked,

frustrated with him. "We either all fight together, or we die separately."

"Tawnie, you need to be careful with these people. The majority of them will accept the challenge of fighting the soldiers at this moment. But they could possibly be high spirited because of your speech."

"Are you saying that I am a good speaker?" My mom asked. Victoria rolled her eyes as she pushed my mother back towards her roaring crowd.

"Hey!" she yelled to quiet the crowd.

"We are involved in a game of cat and mouse that seems to only stop whenever there is nobody in Rexburg alive."

"What do you suggest we do?" Tarker asked.

"We need guns! Lots of them!" She said as she stepped down for a moment to grab the radio that fell to the ground. "If we can hold off in here until the army is ready to make their move, we can ambush them when they come."

"I can get my gang to get you a map of the roads, and we can use the buildings as cover," Tarker suggested.

"Tonight, we just need the guns. There is nothing we could do in the dark." My mother said as she got back up on the bench. "Everybody, get some rest. Tomorrow, we make our stand. We will not die without a fight!" Everyone cheered for a moment, which felt a lot better than the usual despair.

"Wait, wait, hold up there, Dr. Simms!" My mother heard from the radio. Everyone got quiet as they waited for her to react to the call.

"Ring, ring, ring… Copy." It was Jacob Maxwell, and he was actually calling for my mom.

"I just wanted to let you know that you are in my sights right now. Well, in my binoculars anyway." I could see her take a big gulp as the fear hit her. But also etched into her face was anger. "I see you down there having a party. I really wish I was invited."

My mother waited for him to stop talking. When he saw that she had no intention to respond, it angered him.

"Over, dammit!" He screamed into the radio.

"What do you want?"

"I wanted to personally tell you that I have something that you want. Or, someone rather."

"Goddammit, Maxwell! What do you want?!"

"You know exactly what I want!" He yelled, suddenly becoming more deranged with a deeper voice. "And since we are acquainted now, you have twenty-four hours from right now to bring my relic. Test me, and I'll come and wipe out each and every one of you Codex junkies."

"If we are Codex junkies, you made us this way."

Maxwell laughed, and my mother smirked.

"We both know that you are not going to allow us to walk away from this." Maxwell got quiet. "But I promise you, Mr. Maxwell. I can't wait until you get your return."

"Looking forward to it."

CHAPTER XXVII

It was late. After the pep rally and Jacob Maxwell's call, everyone had scattered to rest for the night. My mother left me with Victoria and her husband. I was long asleep while my mom and Officer Gordon took watch. The two of them were finally getting a chance to speak one on one.

They both sat atop a nearby rooftop, watching the soldiers in the distance.

"So, what's been happening to you lately?" Gordon asked her. She looked over to him, unsure of the many ways in which she could answer the question.

"You have me worried most of the time. That's the only reason I'm asking." He continued.

"It's just... a lot is happening to me right now." She finally responded.

"I understand. I have to say that it's impressive that you've held it straight during this time. Taking care of M.J., looking for Milo, and surviving what seems to be the darkest of times."

She looked back over to him in the dim light and smiled.

"Thank you for saying that," She said to him as she reached over to gently caress his arm. Then she leaned towards him and placed her head on his shoulder. "But I wouldn't have survived this long without you keeping me safe."

Gordon looked at her. She lifted her head again, and they locked eyes, staring at one another for a moment.

"Why do you hate Milo so much?" Gordon asked, breaking the silence. Immediately snapping my mother back to reality. Shocked at the question and the timing, she sat back upright and cleared her throat.

"Milo and I have had problems in our relationship since M.J. was born." She said.

"Why, what happened?"

"I... I'm not sure. Six years ago, when I got pregnant, I realized that he spent most of his time at work."

Gordon turned towards her and paid close attention to her story.

"He left me alone, swollen from carrying his child. He ripped me away from my family for his own personal benefit."

"That's terrible," Gordon said. My mom's head fell as her mind ran through the darker days of her marriage.

"The more I think about it, the angrier it makes me."

"So nothing changed since?" Gordon asked.

"No... things have gotten a lot worse."

"How so?"

My mom paused for a moment to wipe her tears.

"When I gave birth to his son, he disappeared for two days."

"When is M.J.'s birthday?" Gordon asked.

"Next week." My mom said.

"What Day?"

"Saturday."

"That was the day we—"

"Yup. That was the day the Pyro Stone was found seven years ago." She said as she held it up between the two of them. It seemed to have a dim light coming from it. It got quiet for a second as Gordon watched the tears pour from my mom's eyes.

"I have spent my entire career exposing men like Jacob Maxwell. The guy that claims to be some prodigy to the world, yet he does things like this. He came for me before I could come to him by planting one of his disciples in my house." My mother explained.

"Do you think that was his goal?"

"To break me psychologically? That was definitely the plan. I wanted to create a world where all people could live in peace. A world where I did not have to live in fear."

"You mean, as a black woman?" He asked. Silently, my mother shook her head.

"Danny, there is something I need to show you. But I need you to promise not to freak out."

He nodded and paid close attention to her. Hesitant, my mother raised her hand, and he was immediately startled.

"Oh!" He said as his jaw fell. My mom's hand began to glow from the inside, and Gordon had become mesmerized. Just as he started to examine, my mother pulled her arm back and hid it. Full of shame, she held her head low as she expected Gordon to run away scared. But instead, he got up and sat behind her. He put his arms around her waist and embraced her. Unsuspecting affection, my mom became spooked.

"Shh. It's okay." He whispered to calm her down. "You want to make the world an equal and safe space for people with powers."

My mother nodded as tears rolled down her face.

Gordon wiped the tears from her eyes and held her tight. She began to relax as she melted in the embrace of a man that was not my father.

"You're not alone, Tawnie." He said to her.

"What?" She asked.

"I know you feel it."

"Feel what?" She asked with a confused grimace on her face.

"People with the caster gene can feel other casters, right?"

"I'm not sure. Is that how it works?"

"I think so? I usually feel other people with powers. But I can't feel yours."

"Wait, what are you saying?" My mother asked as she turned to look at Gordon.

"The day I was assigned that mission, the government experimented on me and turned me into what I once called a monster."

"You have powers?" she asked with excitement.

"The scientists called me a caster too."

"So, are you like me?"

However, Gordon didn't even hear the question. He began to look into his past, and it crippled him in thought.

"Danny!" she yelled.

"Huh?" He finally came back.

"What happened?" She asked. "Where did you go?"

"I can't say. Some things are best left in the past. But I am willing to do anything that it takes to help you and get out of this mess."

My mother became excited again as she became gleeful.

"Alright, what can you do?"

Meanwhile, on the edge of town, Jacob Maxwell found himself on a video call with a mysterious dark figure at a hotel up the road.

"Did you retrieve it yet?" The deep voice of the person asked from the computer.

"I did not. My apologies, My Lord." Jacob answered.

"You fool!" his voice boomed. "The longer that the relic is not in our hands, the more vulnerable we are!"

"I am aware, My Lord. It was a minor setback, but I assure you that I will get your relic back soon enough. We have come across a few obstacles in the process."

"What obstacles could have stopped an entire army?" The man asked.

"There is a woman who seems to be adamant about stopping me. She has the Pyro Stone at this moment, but she has absolutely no idea what she has in her possession."

The man roared, making the ground shake underneath Maxwell's seat. Fear struck him as he looked around. "Anyone that holds that stone possesses the power of a titan! If you don't get it back, you could lose everything that we have worked for!"

"I assure you, My Lord, we have a plan." Maxwell pleaded.

"I will be watching you, Jacob Maxwell." The dark figure said. "If you fail me once more, I will erase you from existence."

A shadow figure moved across the wall in front of him, and outside of the computer speakers, he heard a voice talking to him.

"Tread carefully, Jacob Maxwell. I'm watching you."

CHAPTER XXVIII

The following day, I awoke to screaming and chaos. I was quickly startled from my sleep on a cold floor underneath a cashier's desk. A dense fog had rolled into the town of Rexburg. There was yelling everywhere outside of the store that we took shelter for the night. We shared this space with many civilians. Those who felt endowed to fight poured out into the parking lot with guns in hand. Fear filled my bones as I peeked out of my hiding spot to look for a familiar face somewhere. In the crowd of people, I could hear the France's giving orders. I tried to call out to them, but I wasn't loud enough to combat the rowdiness of the establishment.

"Everyone remain calm!" Victoria yelled as she guided people out of the door. I looked around to see there were primarily women and children left inside. I could see kids my age crying and screaming as the fighting began. It wasn't long before the gunshots were heard. With each round of bullets, the crowd roared even more.

"Daddy!" A young girl screamed as she broke away from a woman who could have been her mother. I wasn't sure.

"Lyric!" The woman yelled as she began to chase after the girl to the front of the store. As she approached me, I jumped out in front to stop her. With me being half her size, it's no wonder she plowed right through me to get outside. Lester and Victoria heard the girl and the woman screaming and turned around to see what was going on. As the girl reached the corridor, Lester grabbed her by the waist and lifted her from the ground.

"I want my daddy!" She screamed as she floated above the concrete floor. At this point, I was getting back up to my feet and saw the woman as she approached the young girl. The girl cried as she was being pulled away from the door. Lester and Victoria both screamed at them like drill sergeants. I tried to walk to the front with my caretakers.

"Milo!" Lester yelled. "Stand back!"

Bullets poured into the store and broke the windows in the front. Glass shattered over everyone close enough. Because I was so short, I was unaffected, and the adults had to hit the floor to avoid getting shot. Lester pulled out a handgun from his side and hurried back to his feet. He pointed out of the window and began to shoot. He emptied his clip and took cover behind the concrete wall again.

"Vick, I'm going out. Stay here!" Lester said as he changed the clip in his gun.

"No, Lester, I'll go." Victoria said to him. The look that Lester gave her was saddening.

"Victoria, hell no! I can't let you do that!" He yelled at his wife as if she was a child. No matter what she said, she couldn't get him to stop yelling at her. "You're going to stay here, and I'm going to handle this and be back, and we are going to live happily ever after!" Victoria grabbed his face and screamed at him.

"Lester! Shut up!" Finally, the irate man clammed up.

"You know that I have to go, love." She said to him as tears ran down her face. Broken, Lester teared up as he stared at his wife, pain etched in his face.

"Victoria, please don't do this!" He cried out as he put his hands on the back of her neck, holding her close. She shook her head as she tried to get away from him. When it seemed like he had no plans of letting her leave, Victoria gave him a kiss and removed his hands. She stood up and looked down at the fear in her husband's eyes.

"Victoria, please don't do this." He cried out.

The Gem State Siege

"I have to." He tried to get up and grab her, but she took a dive out the window above him. He hurried to his feet and looked for his wife in the fog.

"Victoria!" He screamed. I saw a light that could not have possibly come from guns. Things started to fly through the air that could not be explained at the time. Cars, trucks, soldiers, and even light poles all soared through the air from the parking lot. A vehicle came sliding into the building and perched on the window sill, blocking the opening. Everyone screamed in terror as it started to get quiet. Just as we all began to relax, more cars slid over to the open window to cover it up even more. Lester ran away from the window and joined me in a cashier's booth as we waited for the end of the fight outside.

"It's going to be okay, Milo. I got you." Lester said with wet eyes that he couldn't seem to stop. It was the biggest lie that I've heard in a while. I could hear a whistling sound outside. I looked up at Lester, and the look on his face suggested that it was the end.

"EVERYONE, GET DOWN!"

Suddenly, there was an explosion outside of the store. The force from the impact was so devastating that it rocked us all. Screaming women and children all turned to muffled moans and groans. When I opened my eyes, it was much brighter. The explosion had ripped the front of the store off, and now we were completely exposed. As the rubble fell from the top of the structure, Lester moved about to check on everyone. At that moment, I felt the most unsettling sensation that I have ever encountered. All logic escaped me as I jumped up from the floor, ran to the front of the store, and headed outside.

"Milo!" Lester yelled as he ran after me out into the battlefield.

The Gem State Siege

The fog was thick and hard to see anything in. It was a horrible time to be having a gunfight. I ran through the parking lot, trying to escape the feeling until I tripped over a ledge and began to roll down what seemed like the side of a mountain. Once I got to the bottom, I landed in water. Because I was so small, I struggled as I kicked my legs and realized that my feet were not touching anything. I reached a piece of rebar that was sticking out of the ground and pulled myself out of the water. I looked around and saw that I was inside a sinkhole. The explosion had created a crater, and I had fallen in. I was surrounded by high dirt and ravaged pavement on all sides. I tried to climb out of the hole by running up the sides and grab onto the ledge. Unfortunately, my legs were not strong enough to make it up. On the second run, I fell and hit my lip on a rock as I slid back down into the crater. I would assume that the explosion cracked a water main, which was not good for me in the slightest. I noticed that the hole was filling up with water and fast. I didn't know how to swim at the time. And I couldn't possibly float until the water reached the surface.

"Help!" I screamed at the top of my lungs, hoping anyone would hear me. "Help! I'm stuck!"

"Hey kid, try again, I'll catch you as you come up!" I heard a man yell from the top. I could see a figure silhouetted in the fog and smoke but could not make out his face. I trusted that I was in good hands and just knew that he wouldn't let me drown in the parking lot. So I ran up the side of the crater once more. But because my feet were slippery and heavy from being wet, it was hard to get to the top. His arm reached down into the hole, and I missed it by a finger's length. When I rolled back, I landed on my back in the shallow water. The man encouraged me to get back up and try again. I jumped back up from the puddle and focused on his hand as my determination drove me up that incline one last time. I caught his hand, and he squeezed tight. I kicked myself up from the wall and was pulled out of the hole.

I ran up the slippery dirt and gravel a total of four times before I was able to make it out. But when I did, I wished that I didn't. As soon as I could actually see who pulled me out of the crater, I became horrified. With an evil grin on his face and a pistol in his hand, was one of the soldiers.

"Hey kid, I think your mommy is looking for you. I'll take you to her." He said with a creepy grin.

"No!" I screamed as I tried to fight away from him. But the large brute pulled me along against my will. "Let me go!"

I screamed, punch, and kick as I cried to get away from him. Once I realized that I could not break his grip, I pulled myself towards him and sank my teeth into his hand, forcing him to let me go. I ran away, tasting the man's blood. I had hoped to create enough space between us so that he could lose me in the fog. But unfortunately, he found me again, grabbed me by my neck, and slammed me down to the ground.

"You little retarded brat!" He screamed as he cocked his fist and punched me in the face. He wanted me to stop moving. So when a grown man punches a five-year-old in the nose, that mission is accomplished pretty easily.

The soldier stood up to check his hand and screamed.

"Stupid brat!" It took him probably about two minutes to calm himself down. "If I'm infected with this virus, kid, I'm going to kill you before they kill me." He said as he picked me up and draped me over his shoulder.

"Let's go find mommy." He joked as he began to walk.

The Gem State Siege

Before his foot came down on the third step, I heard a gunshot in the distance. I could feel the soldier drop to his knees and let me go. I fell off to the side and landed on my back next to him. Another silhouette approached out of the fog slowly. I struggled to get up just in case I needed to make a run for it. But I saw the shirt that Lester was wearing. As he approached, the man laughed. He started to say something, but Lester relentlessly shot him in the forehead at point-blank range. The body fell next to me, and I looked down at him. I jumped from the ground and ran to Lester with tears in my eyes. I wrapped my arms around his legs, and silently, he placed his warm hand on the back of my neck.

CHAPTER XXIX

At the edge of town, my mother, Gordon, and the civilians fought to raid Jacob Maxwell's lair. The base of operation was a heavily guarded tent surrounded by a few black-armored SUVs. My mother made it her mission to catch up to the tyrant. They took cover behind a line of cars as they took heavy fire from wave after wave of armed soldiers. They were in the worst of the fight as it seemed like they were not going to make it out.

"Gordon!" My mother called out as the gunshots from downrange pierced the glass of the cars. "I don't think we can take them!"

"It's not over yet!" He yelled at her as he jumped up to start shooting back. Other civilians began to follow up. As the soldiers slowed down fire, Gordon jumped over the car and moved a little closer.

"Move in! Go, go, go!" He yelled as he led the troops into the field.

My mother flanked the right side of the field where more soldiers approached. It seemed like they were succeeding at making their way to the destination to the naked eye. They had not realized that the soldiers who bordered the city's opposite side were closing in on them.

"Where are our reinforcements?!" Gordon yelled.

"I don't know!" she screamed back. "What now?"

Gordon looked at my mother with a look of contentment on his face.

"Gordon, what the hell is wrong with you?" She asked.

"I just want to say that if this is the end, I'm glad to have finally met a woman that I wanted to get better for." He said to her as he dropped his gun.

"Gordon, no! Don't talk like this right now, please!" My mom pleaded with him.

"I just wish I had met you sooner in life, Tawnie Everwood."

"Wait, what are you doing, Gordon?"

My mom grabbed on to him while he stood up in the middle of a gunfight.

"No, you are not going out like that, Danny!"

He went back to her side for a moment and kissed my mother goodbye.

"We'll find your husband and bring him back. I promise." He said as he tried to run off again. He got back down and grabbed her hands to release them. "I love you."

Suddenly, Gordon's entire body began to glow a bright blue light. He smiled big as he jumped up into the air. My mom could see a bright red light in the distance and grew fascinated as it drew closer and fast. A figure cut through the fog attached to the red light and jumped over the car my mom took cover behind. It was Victoria. She jumped up to look and see what was happening and immediately became awestruck. The bright blue ball of light was bouncing back and forth between its targets and Victoria. It was almost like she was playing racketball as she dodged bullets in the middle of the field. It appears as if Gordon and Victoria had abilities that react to one another's. Gordon's powers allowed him to cloak himself inside a ball of energy. He could be used as a weapon by Victoria, who seemed to be telekinetic. My mother found herself relieved as she could finally say that she was not the only reason this chaos was happening. It's kind of grim, but I could understand the feeling.

"Woah." She said as she watched the miraculous events

taking place in front of her. In a matter of seconds, they destroyed vehicles and defeated the firing squad.

The more she watched the fight, the more inspired my mother became. She allowed the two former soldiers to fight as she went out into the field to face Jacob Maxwell. Gordon and Victoria were both able to cover my mother as she ran into the area with her guns up. As she arrived at the base tucked away in the fields, she wondered what surprises await her in the small camp. She pointed her weapon into the base of operation as she stepped toward it with caution.

She entered between the cars, ready to shoot any surprises that popped out in her path. Before she could get to the tent affixed between the four vehicles, bullets began to fly towards her. She managed to jump around the car for cover and hideaway.
"No! No! No!" She heard Jacob Maxwell screaming from inside. "You were not supposed to get this close!"
"It's over, Maxwell! I'm not leaving here without your head and my husband!" My mother yelled out to him.
"Ha!" He yelled back. "Even if you defeat me, Tawnie, you will not defeat what's coming."

My father was tied to a rolling office chair inside the tent in the space set up like an office. My dad was severely beaten and gagged so that he could not talk. He watched Jacob pace around the tent, and at some point, he could see my mom outside through slits in the fabric. Fortunately, Jacob didn't. He heard a sound outside and began to shoot in a panic.
"What did you expect here, Jacob?" He heard my mother ask. "Did you expect to kill us all off and take back the Pyro Stone? What did you want with it?"

The Gem State Siege

"I will tell my plan to your dead body!" He yelled out to her as she stalked him from outside.

"You still want to create that army of super villains, huh?"

"Give me my relic!" He yelled as he shot at a random shadow. A clink was heard as he assumed that my mother had been hit. Dropping his guard, Jacob Maxwell walked over to that side of the tent and swung the fabric up over his head. My father rolled to Jacob and kicked him in the genitals. As he reeled in pain from the impact, Jacob was kicked back to the vehicle outside the tent. As soon as his back was against the truck, my mother went in for the final strike. She had finally gotten her hands on him. Her first move was getting the gun out of his hand, which took little effort. She then beat the spoon-fed rich boy into the ground. When he became incapacitated, she stood back up, loaded a round into the chamber of the gun, and pointed it straight at Jacob's head. But for some reason, she did not pull the trigger. Hesitation hit her at a moment that could have ended it all. But like a villain, Jacob laughed at her.

"What the hell is so funny, jackass?" My mom asked.

"You think it's over, Tawnie?" He asked before spitting blood out of his mouth. "You and I are just getting started."

"What are you talking about?"

Soldiers started to pour in to get the drop on my mom. She took a deep breath and closed her eyes for a moment as she slowly raised her hands in defeat.

"I highly advise you to put the gun down, Caster." One of the soldiers commanded her. Jacob, still laughing, picked himself up from the ground while another grabbed my mother. They pushed her out into the field, facing the city. At this point, the battle had stopped. She looked at a line of nothing but soldiers in the distance. Not far from her, Gordon

The Gem State Siege

and Victoria sat on their knees with their hands behind them. Not far from them were Lester and me. There were also civilians in the middle of this sitting with guns pointed at them as well. The expression on my mother's face slowly changed as hope for victory faded.

"This is great!" Jacob laughed as he pulled the handgun from a nearby soldier's waist and walked over to me. "This is so great!"

"Hey!" My mother called out to him as he indulged in his maniacal celebration and could not even hear her. "HEY!" Finally, he looked over to her. The soldier behind my mom dug the cold steel of the barrel into her scalp.

"Don't do this. I'll give you what you want." My mom said to him, making everyone call out in resounding objection.

"Is that so? Where exactly is my Pyro Stone?"

"Are you crazy? I will not tell you where it is when you have this much leverage."

Jacob stopped what he was doing and switched gears for a moment as he looked around. His playful side had vanished once more, and it was back to business. He walked over to her and leaned over to get at eye level.

"I suggest you not play with me, Tawnie. You know what I am capable of." He cautioned her.

"I do."

A soldier rolled my father out from the tent, and Jacob punched her. My father mumbled through the gag in his mouth as he struggled to break free of the ropes that bound him to the chair.

"I wonder," Jacob said as he looked around at all the people. I remember watching him as the tyrant looked at me. I felt chills through my entire body as he stared with only

God knows what in his mind.

"I wonder, how many of these people I'll have to kill for you to cooperate, Tawnie." He said as he walked across the grass, straight towards me. My eyes grew large as I tried to get away from the soldier that was holding me.

"No, no, no!" I screamed. "Mommy!"

"Mommy and daddy can't save you now, tiny Milo." He said to me as he raised his gun.

"Jacob!" My mom screamed out to him. My dad still squirming in the chair.

"Say goodbye, kid." I helplessly watched as Maxwell placed his index finger on the trigger of the gun

The pause at that moment was unbearable and seemed like it lasted forever. There was no bluff in this monster at all. I could feel myself go black as I heard the gun go off. However, I didn't feel anything. I listened to my mother shriek in horror, and there was crying from next to me. As my head was turned to her. I opened my eyes to Victoria sobbing as she looked at the ground in front of me. I looked and saw Gordon's body. He gargled blood and began to bleed out in front of us, and we couldn't do anything about it. As we watched him take his last breath, Jacob immediately unleashed the second shot. This time, right between Lester's eyes, killing him instantly. Victoria screamed as she jumped over to her husband's body.

My mother had finally seen enough. She was now angry enough to literally explode. She began to glow and blast light from her hands at any soldier standing in her line of sight. As the blasts hit them, their bodies burned away like tobacco ashes. I took cover behind Gordon's body as the gunfight started again. Every soldier in this field used my mom and dad as target practice. She was hit by a bullet and took a fall

The Gem State Siege

as she expelled energy to create a shield to protect them. I could see her struggling to hold the shield up, and my dad still worked to release himself from the ropes.

    I put my head back down and cried as I assumed this was the end. Until I looked at Gordon's shackled wrists and noticed that he had something clenched in his fists. I pried his grip on whatever it was and eventually got his fingers open. Inside his hands was the glowing Pyro Stone. I picked it up and raised it into the air, looking at it in the light. Maxwell dashed toward me, his eyes locked on his prize.

    "Milo, no!" My mother screamed as she reached for me. Remember that feeling that I explained earlier? That feeling like something was coming? The feeling that I ran from on the I-15? It turns out that I, myself, am a Caster, and I could feel my own energy. But of course, as a five-year-old with no training, I couldn't possibly know that. All I knew was, it was warm all of a sudden. The world around me began to look familiar as walls of fire shot up into the sky. It was the same power that destroyed Idaho Falls, and it was now happening again. It was me this entire time. My mother knew what I did, and she did her best to protect me. She knew that if I had the Pyro Stone it would happen again. But she couldn't be helped now. Nobody could.

    That day ended with a quiet battlefield. Smoke from the scorched remains of the survivors of The Gem State Siege rose into the sky. On that day, three things were created: The Savior, The Catalyst, and The Destroyer. I've spent my entire life up until this point trying to figure out which one I am.

CHAPTER XXX

The days to follow were chaotic. People nationwide wondered what happened to friends and loved ones in Idaho and its bordering states. The tragic explosion seemed to shake the entire world. News of the Codex Virus spilled as the government covered up those tragic events by calling it a natural disaster. Some news outlets said that there were chemicals in the crops that caused people to get ill. This created the nationwide scarcity of produce grown in Idaho. Some so-called "woke" news outlets even went as far as to say that it was a race war gone wrong. But this only proves how much media propaganda is part of the problem.

Vice President McTierman sat in a room underneath The White House after declaring a state of emergency. He was heavily guarded in the catacombs of Lower D.C. But the city above was in outrage. Who could blame them, though? You think you're free until you are not welcomed to information that affects your life and how you make decisions. When you are the face of a government once strong and mighty, when it collapses, you become the leader that destroyed everything. This was the position of the Vice President, who was now our new Commander and Chief.

Chief of Staff, Mr. Waddell, entered the room with a man that, for now, we will call, The Cleaner. The two men sat down at the table with The President at the head. Waddell introduced the associate, and the President began to clam up in his speech. The intimidating man with eyes that showed no emotion stared at The President in silence.

The Gem State Siege

"A tricky situation you have here, Mr. Vice President." The shady man in the three-piece suit said.

"Yes, I'm aware."

"I also hear that congratulations are in order. Heard you are going to be succeeding our late President. Must be an exciting time for you."

"Actually, it's a bit bittersweet because I lost a good friend and brother on the way."

"Right, I suppose so. Now, for the problem at hand." The man said as he leaned forward. He put his elbows on the table and interlocked his fingers while staring at the men across the table. "How are we going to explain the catastrophe in Idaho? And don't feed me some bull shit. My boss won't like that very much."

"It is our understanding that the events that took place in Idaho were a result of a chemical contamination," Waddell said. The man sighed loudly.

"You guys could not even get two minutes into the conversation without telling me a lie." The Cleaner said to them. The President and his Chief of Staff looked at one another in panic. They both stammered over one another to speak.

"Mister..."

"My name is not important. The only name that matters is his." The Cleaner told Waddell.

"I'm sorry, who are you talking about, now?" McTierman asked.

"Mr. Vice President. The man in your position is obligated to serve, honor, and protect on the highest level. You are responsible for protecting the constitution and holding the gold standard of what this government is supposed to be. I sure do hope that you gentlemen are keeping your integrity."

The Gem State Siege

"Are you accusing the American President of treason?" McTierman asked.

"Mr. Vice President, I haven't made an accusation yet. But if I continue gathering evidence that points to individual parties, then I must do my job. No hard feelings." The room immediately became tense.

"Do you understand that... Sir?" The Cleaner taunted the two men.

"How dare you patronize me?" Vice President McTierman screamed as he jumped up from his seat. However, The Cleaner remained calm with a grin on his face. Once The President threw his tantrum, The Cleaner laughed. He stood up from his chair, adjusted his necktie, and put his hands behind his back. He gave The President a cold stare as they all got quiet.

"Mr. President, I assure you that your title is not important in this matter. So throwing your weight isn't wise during our ongoing investigation." McTierman was baffled that the man would be as gutsy.

"You must be a man with a death wish," Waddell said to him.

"Mr. Waddell, I am not here to cause trouble. I simply want answers. The answers that every citizen deserves and to make sure that justice is served." The Cleaner said to him.

"Guards!" The Vice President called out. Two members of the secret service opened the heavy metal door and entered the room with force.

"Guards, get this man out of my sight!" The Vice President demanded. Still, The Cleaner stood in his spot and stared at the Vice President. The Secret Service Members seemed to have been frozen by fear as they both stared at the mysterious man.

The Gem State Siege

"Hmm, interesting. They saw me and immediately lost your order like a sketchy drive-through. I wonder why that is."

The Cleaner headed to the door and stopped in between the two Servicemen. He looked at both of them and then over his shoulder to the Vice President.

"I was hoping that you guys could be cleared of your role as suspects of this investigation. But, he will hear all about this. And he is not a patient man. Isn't that right, fellas?" He asked the servicemen. However, they did not answer.

The mysterious man was escorted out of the room. McTierman got up to head to the other side of the table, where a glass decanter sat atop a small table against the wall. He picked up the bottle and two glasses. Hands shaking uncontrollably, he poured one drink, not without spilling any of the brown liquid on the surface of the table. Waddell became concerned and raised an eyebrow as he heard the alcoholic beverage splash onto the hard concrete floor. McTierman put the bottle back down. He then looked back at Waddell as sweat began to drip from his brow.

"Mr. Vice President, you don't look so good," he said. McTierman then looked back at the decanter and picked the bottle up as well as the glass. He walked both back to the table and sat at his chair. He looked at the cup and slid it across the table to Waddell. He then proceeded to tilt the entire bottle to his lips and drank.

"Mr. Vice President, what's going on."

"Mr. Waddell, if those guys are coming for me, I won't win." He ominously stated with no context at all.

"Who?" Waddell asked.

"How much time you got?"

The Gem State Siege

Meanwhile, a helicopter lands at a Primotech facility in Northern California. Spectators stood by waiting as the passengers of the vehicle unloaded. Fans and reporters from news mediums all over stood in high anticipation. The helicopter shut down, and it had gotten silent in the parking lot of the massive research facility. The door opened, and a few black-clad soldiers jumped out of the vehicle. Following the armed detail was none other than the man himself, Jacob Maxwell. I still don't know how that monster survived an explosion that took hundreds of lives until this day. Being right in the middle of the blast, it was almost impossible. He had suffered a few minor burns and bruising, but he had somehow made it out unscathed.

He followed his security detail down the runway and headed into the facility. Lights flashing as paparazzi snapped photos from all angles. Rioters outside the parking lot seemed to already have a clue as to what was going on. That will make sense later.

"Mr. Maxwell, what happened in Rexburg?" One reporter asked, pointing a microphone in Jacob's face.

"Mr. Maxwell, any word on the rumor that there is a virus coming?" Another asked in the same fashion. The guards nudged the reporters to the side as they cleared a path for Jacob to get to the building. Once they got inside the long tunnel of bystanders, the crowd swarmed Maxwell. The two guards did their best to keep him safe as they continued to inch towards the door. All things were good until one of the paparazzi got physical with the guard causing a fight to break out. Jacob used the commotion to duck away and escape the crowd. After about five minutes of pandemonium, he finally reached the building's secure entrance. As he fumbled with a biometric scanner on the door, he was discovered by the crowd. Once again, they swarmed and backed him into a corner.

"Mr. Maxwell, do you deny allegations of your involvement with the catastrophe in Idaho?" A reporter questioned.

"Mr. Maxwell, how do you feel about being a suspect in the terrorist attack in Idaho Falls?" Asked another. Suddenly, the door swung open, and Maxwell scurried inside like a mouse. The reporters boldly ran to the door, trying to enter the facility. But they were shocked by tasers from the building's armed guards. Eventually, they were able to close the door behind him.

Just as he started to collapse against the wall, the guards caught Maxwell and began to walk him back to his office. Once they arrived at the top floor office, they walked Jacob over to his desk and sat him down in his chair. The light of the sun beamed in and splashed against him.

"Close the damn blinds!" He demanded. His assistant, a young woman, hustled over to the button that closed the shades. After the heat he endured in Rexburg, it's no wonder he was retaliating against sunshine.

"Mr. Maxwell, you should be at home resting." The young assistant said to him.

"I can't. I have work that needs to be done." He said as he proceeded to look through his desk drawers for something.

"But you shouldn't sacrifice your health in the process, sir."

Maxwell lifted his head and looked at the woman with disdain in his eyes. Fear ran through her body as she made eye contact with him. His deranged look had trapped her in fear. After about ten seconds of staring, she finally began to back away slowly. She reached for the door handle, still looking at him.

"Let me know if you need anything, Mr. Ma--"

"GET OUT!" He screamed, cutting the overly caring woman off. Without another word, the woman bolted out of his office, leaving him to start his pity party.

Jacob put his head down on his desk and closed his eyes for a minute. He just wanted to relax at his office before he started to get back into the swing of working. But the time for rest was taken away from him by an unexpected guest.

"Mr. Maxwell!" A young brunette woman in a black pantsuit sat in a chair in front of Maxwell's desk.

"Aaah!" He screamed after lifting his head and laying eyes on the sexy businesswoman. He reached down into the bottom drawer of his desk and pulled out a handgun. He looked the green-eyed woman in the eyes and noticed that she had no fear in her expression. She grinned at his efforts to intimidate her.

"Now, now, Jacob, put that away. We both know exactly why you're not going to use it."

"Who...who...who are you? And how did you get... when did you get in here?" He stammered.

"Who I am is not important. But you can call me... Fixer." She said as she leaned back in the chair.

"What do you want?" Jacob asked as he put his gun down on the desktop.

"It doesn't matter what I want. But 'He' wants answers because someone has been a bad, bad boy. I'm only here to find out who."

"Who is 'He,'" Jacob asked.

"You shall find out soon enough, Mr. Maxwell." The

woman said as she stood up from the chair.

She crossed her arms and began to pace the hard tile floor with her high heels clicking with each step. At first, her eyes were forward, then she looked at Jacob from the corner of her eyes. When she stopped, she turned to face him.
"I need you to be honest during this conversation, Mr. Maxwell. I will go out on a limb to say that you are a good man based on your work. I would much rather reveal you to have had nothing to do with this."
"Okay, what do you want to know?" He asked in confidence.
"What happened in Idaho last week?"
"What didn't happen there last week? He sarcastically asked.
"Answer the question, Mr. Maxwell!" Suddenly, he retreated and clammed up in his chair, waiting for her to ask it again.
"What happened in Rexburg?

Jacob began to space out as he thought back on the events that took place just a week prior.
"Yes, recollect all those memories for me. Paint the picture."
"I was in Rexburg when the catastrophe happened." He said.
"I know that already. Why were you there?"
"I was passing through, coming from Yellowstone."
"How did you escape?" The woman asked him. Finally, Maxwell snapped as he grew tired of being bombarded with questions.
"I will not answer any more questions, Ms. Fixer or whoever you are!" He yelled, sticking out his chest to seem

tough.

"That's fine," Fixer said as she approached his desk once more. Paranoid, Jacob grabbed the gun again and pointed it at the young lady. She raised her hands and bent over to grab her purse.

"Get out!" He snarled.

Fixer turned to the door and walked towards it. Before she could reach out to touch the handle, Fixer looked back at him.

"May the Gods have mercy on your soul, Mr. Maxwell." She said to him.

"Wait. What did you say?"

"I'm going to pray for you, Mr. Maxwell. You're going to need it for what's coming for you."

CHAPTER XXXI

As days passed, the media portrayed Jacob Maxwell as some sort of hero. He capitalized on our misery, saying that he tried to rescue people. He crossed the line by saying that the good people who stood against him were the terrorist, and he was innocent. He was revered as a hero. Somehow, the names of my people had been slandered as the villains of this story. The worst part of it all was that nobody was there to stop it. Jacob Maxwell could say whatever he wanted and get away with it all. Why not? All of the evidence was burned to the ground.

The city of Seattle held a ceremony to honor this tyrant as the man that helped stop a terrorist attack. They managed to put together an entire black-tie event with him as the guest of honor. Also in attendance, the newly elected President McTierman and his Vice President, Henry Waddell. The city, on the night of the event, was cold and rainy. It had been clear skies all day up until the time that the guests started to arrive at this little shindig. Despite the thunderstorm, city officials urged the staff to proceed with the event. The way they handled it, there was nothing that could stop this celebration.

As the United States President arrived, he hopped out of his service vehicle on the red carpet with his wife. Not far behind were the secret servicemen that met him to enter the facility. They walked through a flood of paparazzi and journalists who all asked a million questions, begging to pose for a million pictures. The President was uneasy the entire way through the venue. But nothing made him as uncomfortable as catching a glimpse of The Cleaner and The Fixer lurking in the crowd. Because of all the photo-ops, The two men couldn't react to seeing the unknown mercenaries. They were forced to endure the fear until they got inside.

As soon as they entered the building, the entire Presidential Party was taken to a back entrance. This protected them from the public eye. This would serve to be an excellent place to hide from the creepy reps of the unknown. Nobody else was allowed in the back.

"Mr. President!" Waddell called out as he walked into the room that the President was in, pacing the floor.

"Yeah, I know. Why the hell are they here?"

"I have no clue, but it can't be anything good." Said Waddell as he wiped the sweat from his brow.

"If they are here to blow our cover, then it's all over."

"I understand, Mr. President. Should we find a way to accidentally make them vanish?" Waddell asked under his breath as he remained cautious of his surroundings.

"I suggest we do it quickly because we are blind to them at this moment. We have no idea what their intentions are, who they work for, or what type of dirt they have." With no hesitation, the President made a call.

"Mr. President!" He heard Jacob from a distance. The President turned around and saw the proclaimed hero and his wife coming right for him.

"Ahh, Mr. Maxwell! Good to see you, my friend!" He greeted the young entrepreneur with a stiff hand extended to him.

"It's been a while, hasn't it?" Maxwell asked.

"It sure has."

"Mr. President, Mr. Maxwell, can we get a photo op?" a

reporter asked.

"Absolutely, the President answered. The two men held on to one another's hand and turned to face the camera. As they smiled big for the photo, there was a conversation in secrecy. While everyone was glad to see The President and the hero together, they had important business to discuss.

"What the hell did you do?" the President asked Maxwell as he continued smiling for the cameras.

"I did nothing that can't be undone in the drop of a hat and the snap of a finger," Maxwell answered.

"I would love to believe that, but you have caught the attention of the wrong group of people. It's not looking good for any of us right now."

"Relax, I made sure that we swept the land clean of anything that leads back to our mission."

"Obviously not!" The President said as he got angry with Maxwell.

"Mr. President, over here!" A paparazzi woman called out to him.

"Okay, gotcha!" He said as he squeezed Maxwell's hand to get him to turn. He wanted to wince in pain, but he held it together as they turned to face the other line of cameras.

"People, there will be plenty of time for photos. If we keep this up, I'll get a tan." The President joked. Everyone began to laugh, and he whispered one last thing into Maxwell's ear that spooked him.

The President walked back over to his Chief of Staff so that they could head to their seats. The show was about to start.

"It's done," Waddell said to the President as a wave of uneasiness rushed over them. They then pulled their wives with them into the seating area of the venue. Cleaner and Fixer both walked around the facility in separate locations. Both of them keeping an eye out on things from the inside. The Cleaner walked out into the building's foyer and lobby area and saw a group of Secret Servicemen scoping him out. Instinctively, Cleaner led the men into a nearby, unused hallway. Near the Galley, Fixer waltzed through, doing the same. She spent some time looking out to the rear of the building for suspicious activity near the dock. As she walked past a door that led to an alley, it swung open, and in came two of the Servicemen. She looked back to acknowledge them and quickly realized that two more were in front of her.

"Good evening, fellas." The woman said to them. "What brings you out tonight?" Without warning, the men attacked her.

Back in the venue's general area, people seated themselves at the many round tables in the auditorium while the ceremony started. The lights faded, and a screen began to light up behind the stage. The Governor of the State of Washington graced the scene, and the crowd started to cheer.

"Alright, everyone, silence your phones, and let's get started!" The host said into the microphone.

"Thank you, thank you!" She started off by saying as she fumbled with the microphone stand on the podium. "I'm glad you all can make it here tonight. I thought we were going to get washed out beforehand, huh?" The crowd began to laugh at her awkward joke as she tried to break the ice before actually speaking.

"For anyone who doesn't know me already, my name is Katdari Singh, and I am the Governor of the beautiful Washington State." Everyone began to cheer again. In the crowd, The President sat at one of the tables directly in front

The Gem State Siege

of the stage. He had a clear view of the neighboring table where many people sat, but he still had a clear picture of Jacob Maxwell. The two men looked at one another with rage in their eyes. Jacob, however, was definitely more afraid than anything.

"We gather here tonight to honor a man that has done so much for this planet that it's safe to assume that he wants to be featured in the Bible." Governor Singh joked. This time the crowd laughed a little more.

"This man has proved to not just this country, but the entire world that he is here to be the living blessing that keeps on protecting and providing for us."

The Governor continued with accolade on top of accolade. The plan was for her to introduce him up to the stage. But lurking behind the scenes were two agents that made the President tremor in fear. As he saw them approach the center of the stage from both sides, he reached over and tapped Waddell. The Cleaner approached the podium with an arrogant demeanor. Fixer scowled at the Governor. The woman stopped talking and looked behind her. She had become startled and cautiously moved out of their way.

"What are you two doing here?" Governor Singh asked the mysterious but nicely dressed thugs. The crowd was shocked at the arrival of the two mercenaries but remained relatively quiet.

"Who is that?"

"What are they doing?"

"What's going on?" All questions you could hear in the semi-quiet room.

"Governor Singh." The unknown mercenary called into the microphone. "Hold on, I'll let you finish. But how you finish is up to you." The crowd began to get antsy as they questioned what was happening.

"You could end this night any way you want. But not until you see the truth."

It was at that moment that a single phone in the audience began to ring. The loud chiming distracted the spectators as one ringing phone turned into an entire room. As the crowd pulled out their phones, a video started on the large screen on stage, and every phone in attendance. The footage showed glitching and static in the opening. It was a self-shot video, and the camera person struggled to get situated. Finally, the camera got steady. The video showed my mother as she sat in front of the camera with tears in her eyes.

"I am recording this video on February 7th, 2020. I am in the middle of the so-called pandemic created by Primotech. We have been running for the past two days and being hunted by soldiers who are ordered to shoot on site. Innocent people have been slaughtered, and the survivors are coping with the fact that nobody will survive. If this video made it to you, then it means that I did not make it."

The crowd began to look around with concern as the video started to show dead bodies on Rexburg's streets. You can then see the headlights of the military vehicles through the fog in the distance. She recorded this video mere seconds before the group of assassins stormed the city.

"Those are the men that will be sweeping in on this city in the next few minutes. I have attached the files that incriminate the organization responsible for this massacre." She explained as she looked out into the fields. "Or should I say, the man that is responsible for this? The man who murdered us all is none other than Jacob Maxwell. All of the men on his assassin's payroll are included. They experimented on us, then decided that we were not fit to survive. I only hope you find this file. You are our only hope for eternal peace."

As she finished that sentence, gunshots could be heard in the background. You could see the fear in my mother's face as she looked out into the distance.

"If you don't catch this monster, so help you, God." Then the laptop she was using was closed. The video was finished, but an audio clip started to play.

"He's always killing people."

"Come on, Tyson, you're a trained killer. Don't tell me that you have a problem with doing your job."

"No, but this is all dangerous, man. What if Primotech found out about this?"

"Then knowing the boss, we would be going to war with them too."

"Do you think he is capable of killing everyone in this state without the government knowing?"

"Doesn't matter. If we fail, then we die. It's simple."

"Is the Pyro Stone really worth that much?"

"Enough to eradicate mankind for."

The crowd was dumbfounded by their revelation of the truth. Everyone began to look at the man that was supposed to be honored as a hero that night. The look on his face was priceless as he noticed all of the eyes that glared at him. Perceptions all over the venue began to change as the reality of Maxwell's crimes caught up to him.

"Now." The Fixer said on the microphone. "Governor Singh, you may continue."

At this moment, Jacob Maxwell tried to make his getaway by heading to the door to escape. But as he reached the door, a group of police officers came in with hands on their pistols.

Governor Singh approached the microphone once more. Fixer came to whisper something in her ear. Governor Singh's expression went from confused to afraid in a matter of a few words.

"Ladies and gentlemen, this event has concluded." She announced.

Jacob Maxwell was indicted and sentenced to life in prison on many counts of terrorism and treason. Every police officer in the country made a game out of hunting down the surviving soldiers he recruited. One would assume that all the world was going back to normal after the tragedies of Rexburg. A fabricated pandemic disappeared. The world started to understand what Jacob Maxwell was trying to achieve. Unfortunately, he had already created something that could not be reversed. Unless there was another group prepared to destroy the entire world. Maxwell being arrested and incarcerated was a start to fixing the overall problem. But there was a bigger conspiracy that caused that event to take place.

Back in the ruins of Rexburg, Idaho, a group of investigators searched the city for more evidence. A lone man walked the shattered city streets as his team searched high and low. But what were they looking for? Who were they? A lucky little boy was about to find out.

"Sir!" A young woman approached the 6'2" man that wore a suit of armor underneath a long black trench coat. The man turned to look at the woman.

"Cadet, what is it?" He questioned with a deep voice.

"Sir, we found the boy. But you have to see this! Come quick!" That is how it all started.

The Gem State Siege

The Gem State Siege

Thank you for taking the time to read my novel "The Gem State Siege". If you enjoyed it, please take the time to review the book online at your favorite outlets, including:

Goodreads
Amazon
Library Thing
Reedsy Discovery
Love Reading
The Millions
SFBook Reviews
Bookpage
Book Riot
Net Galley
Book Bub

Your review helps with getting excited readers to see the book and let others know what happened to Tawnie! You know, so help everyone else find out.

Side note: This is the best way to do it without spoiling the story… Thank You!!!

The Gem State Siege

Next, in The World's End Series:
The Guardian of the Pacific

I stared at him for a moment, then looked around at all the others. I honestly thought it was a prank of some sort. So I hesitated to grab it from his hand.
"Shame," Mr. Wiley said from the bridge. "The boy is so traumatized he won't even accept a real gift."
"I think you're right cap," Said Chad. "Luke, take the bait."
"Do I have to?" I asked as I stepped back from the bag. "You guys probably have a glitter bomb in there like last time."
"Luke, it's your birthday for crying out loud! Take the bag before I put it in the net with the trash!" Chad demanded as he snatched the sparkling, blue bag away from Malcolm.
"You better not!" Kiyanna yelled at him as she then snatched the bag from him. "Luke, we all pitched in to get you something nice for your birthday,"

Kiyanna stepped forward and handed me the bag with a smile that held a little bit of sorrow behind it. It was almost like she felt sorry for me. Chad and Malcolm smiled with her as they all stared, waiting for me to take it. Still, I declined.
"Guys, that's incredibly nice of you, but I'm okay." I said to them.
"Luke, seriously! Just take the bag already!" Kiyanna yelled while the guys groaned in annoyance.
"Guys, this isn't about the gift." I said to them. The three

of them got quiet for a moment. "I'm fine. I promise."
I walked away from Kiyanna, leaving her with the gift bag. Her head fell as she took the gift back into the lower deck of boat. Malcolm and Chad both looked at me with concern on their faces before walking away to do something else. I sat next to Laura who was quietly reading a book about a mermaid princess or something. She looked up at me, then smiled. Her book closed on her thumb to keep her page as she reached over to touch the back of my hand.

Blue suddenly came from the lower deck with her tail pointing straight out.
"What the?" I said to myself as I watched the dog head over to the railing along the side of the boat. She began to bark. It was as if she had seen something.
"Happy birthday, Lucas." Laura said to me. Startled, I stared at her, feeling myself starting to turn red.
"Uh... Thanks Laura." I bashfully responded. I looked back over at Blue and stood to go see what was going on. Laura got up to follow.
"What's happening?" Chad asked.
"I don't know," said Mr. Wiley. "She never acts like this."
"Blue, what's wrong girl?" I asked as I pat her head gently. Suddenly, I began to see the trash in front of me rise. Mr. Wiley began to look concerned as he stared with horror on his face.
"Mr. Wiley, what's happening?"
"EVERYBODY, HANG ON!" He screamed as he frantically pushed Laura and I to the center of the boat.

He made a run for Blue. But before he could reach her, a hard jolt rocked the boat and a wall of water and trash ascended into the sky in front of us. Laura slipped and hit her head on the deck and now seemed incoherent. I grabbed hold of her as the entire vessel started to capsize. I held on for dear life with one hand on the leg of the bench and my other hand gripping Laura's drenched t-shirt. I could see the waves crashing against the deck that was now completely vertical. At this point, I was losing my grip. Miraculously, we started to fall in the right direction, but it was too late…

Join my mailing list to stay up to date on the latest news about The Guardian of the Pacific!

Want to pre-order the book now? Visit www.ajmcmullen.com/books.

The Gem State Siege

Want to spend less on "The Guardian of the Pacific?" Here's your chance!

Now we play a game of trivia. If you can get the answer, you will get access to 50% off when you purchase book 2 of The World's End Series. Don't worry, the question is not a hard one. But let's see if you were paying attention.

In The Gem Stat Siege, Tawnie Simms recorded a video to use as evidence against Jacob Maxwell. If you can recall the exact date that this video was recorded, you will get your prize!

When you have the answer, enter it in the discount code section for book 2 when you purchase at ajmcmullen.com (MMDDYYY). Or email us at info@ajmcmullen.com.

If you are interested in more content from the author, then you MUST join my mailing list today! From short stories, discounts, promotions, and news about upcoming content—be the FIRST to know!

Subscribe TODAY at ajmcmullen.com!

ABOUT THE AUTHOR

AJ McMullen, born in September 1990, has a sharp eye for creativity. Breeding himself to become a hip-hop artist, he always had the talent of writing and producing music; which has now become his hobbies. He began writing in the 5th grade when he and a group of childhood friends wrote anime Fanfiction of a beloved and popular TV series. However, he was never able to put the pen down again.

AJ has since written many stories over the span of his career that has never been published or talked about. But the universe that he was able to create has always been a staple conversation and dropped jaws since the beginning of the project. A man who feels that it is his duty to let the world see his inner thoughts, he has become self-obligated to finish what he started. And that is the Ascension Universe.

Read more on my website www.ajmcmullen.com

The Gem State Siege

Bibliography

-Written Works-
The Gem State Siege • S0B2 • S0B3 • S1B1

-Remainder of The World's End Series-
S0B4 • S0B5 • S0B3 • S0B4 • S0B5 • S0B6 • S0B7 • S0B8 • S0B9 • S0BX

-Future Projects-
S1B1 • S1B2 •S1B3 • S1B4

-Upcoming Serial-
Ventross-Weekly Release (For Patreons ONLY! For preview, join my mailing list where episodes release bi-weekly)

All upcoming titles have been Withd with Ascension SKU Numbers to prevent spoilers in the series. Subscribe to my mailing list to be the first to know about upcoming changes to these titles!

The Ventross Series is a bi-weekly, episodic release exclusively for Patreon members with the appropriate tier. Your contributions to Patreon and AJ McMullen will help fund more content and faster releases. Thank you for your support!

SUPPORT THE AUTHOR

CHECK ME OUT ON PATREON!

Please come show your support on Patreon! I'm not asking you for donations! There is a lot more content there to be seen. From behind the scenes, to illustrations, to exclusive never-before-seen content, find it all on patreon.com/ajmcmullen.

Made in the USA
Coppell, TX
12 April 2021